# THE BOYFRIEND

## DANIEL HURST

INKUBATOR
BOOKS

# PROLOGUE

These old trees have seen a lot over the years. Forming the woods that loom large over this town, they are just as much a part of the local area as the shopping centre, the cinema and the cosy Italian restaurant where diners can get fifty percent off on a Tuesday. And just like those places, they make an excellent choice for lovers to visit and spend time together.

Many couples have come here over the years, walking hand in hand amongst the tall trunks, laughing and joking about the future and what it might bring. Some have even stopped to scratch their names into the bark, two sets of initials surrounded by a love heart, a tradition to declare that this is a love that will stand the test of time.

Ten minutes in these woods, and you would think that the world is full of lovers.

But you would be wrong.

It's full of exes too, those unlucky few who weren't blessed with everlasting love and instead suffered the pain of their relationship ending when once it had seemed like it would go on forever. Many of those initials remain on the trees, their removal hardly a priority for broken-hearted people who find themselves single once again. While once the existence of the engravings proved that the world was a beautiful place, now they are simple reminders that not everything goes to plan, and pain and misery are just as much a part of love as happiness and contentment.

There are too many trees and too many love hearts in these woods for walkers to pay attention to them all. But one day, one of these trees demanded attention, and it was impossible to ignore.

The body hung from a rope that was tied around the branch of an ancient oak tree. It was a male, mid-thirties, and although he would be easily identified in good time by the local police and his grief-stricken family members, there was rather a large hint just behind him.

It was on the bark of the tree that he was suspended from where a message had been carved into the wood. There were two initials framed by a love heart, faded over time but still readable.

*SG & AD 4eva.*

SG was this man, hanging from the branch.

AD was his former lover, who would be shocked by the news of his death, as well as deeply saddened.

But there had been somebody else at the scene, a person who had been far too smart to leave clues to their name lying around in a place like this.

This wasn't a tree where a man had committed suicide, even though that was exactly what it had been made to look like.

This was a tree where a murder victim hung.

And the killer was only just getting started…

# 1

'Hi. I have a table booked for eight o'clock under Adele Davies.'

I wait patiently for the pretty waitress to double-check the screen in front of her before she gives me a smile and grabs a couple of drinks menus.

'Follow me, Adele.'

She leads me away from the front door and deeper into the venue, which is already full of thirsty patrons who are seated and enjoying their beverages amongst the low lighting and elegant sounds of a piano player in the far corner. This is my first time here, and the booking was a result of my best friend's suggestion, but I can already tell that it was a good idea. It's certainly a classy establishment, and not just because there is a guy in a tuxedo tickling the ivories. Everything from the dress code of the waiters and waitresses to the presentation of the colourful drinks is immaculate, and the flickering candles, wood-panelled bar and plush leather seats only add further prestige to this cosy venue in the heart of Manchester city centre.

Whoever said it was grim up north had obviously never been in here.

I smile at the waitress as she shows me to my table, accepting the menus and settling down into my luxurious seat before checking the time and wondering how long Nicola is going to be. It's not that I mind her being late – I've certainly been guilty of such a sin several times in our friendship. But I am eager for her to get here because we do have rather a lot to talk about, and the sooner we get started, the less chance there is of me being late home again and drawing the ire of my fiancé.

Tom isn't a strict partner by any means and is more than happy for me to go and enjoy myself with friends whenever I like. What he doesn't like so much is when I tell him that I won't be late home or that I'll be limiting myself to one or two drinks, only to stagger through the front door at midnight, singing loudly while carrying some disgusting box of takeaway food.

Especially on a weeknight when we both have to be up at dawn.

Tonight has been another one of those times where I have perhaps rather stupidly told him that I would be home at a decent hour and in an appropriate state, although now that I'm here with a tempting menu of cocktails in my hand, I can easily see myself staying for a while. And the later Nicola is in getting here, the later I will be in getting home.

I'm considering going ahead and ordering a drink without her, because I can see the waitress hovering nearby, when Nicola enters the room and gives me a wave as she rushes past all the tables in the direction of our own.

'Sorry I'm late! Got stuck in a meeting! Thought it would never end!'

I tell her not to worry about it as I stand and give her

a hug before retaking my seat and feeling my body sink back into the comfortable material.

'If I'd known it was going to be this posh, I'd have worn something a little more fashionable,' I say, referring to the plain blouse I have on after a day in the office at the accounting firm I work for.

'Don't be silly. You look gorgeous as always,' Nicola tells me rather kindly before running her fingers through her dark hair. 'I look like a bloody gargoyle next to you.'

I laugh at my friend's self-deprecating joke, although I wish she wouldn't put herself down. But she's always been like that ever since I've known her, which has been twenty-five years now, mind-bogglingly enough.

We met on the first day of secondary school, although it was actually the 'misfortune' of a clerical error that led to us doing so. Before starting at the school, pupils had been able to nominate one other person who they wished to be paired with so that they could ease into the new surroundings with their best friend by their side. I had nominated a girl called Rachel Evans, who had been my best friend at primary, but it was only when I walked into class on that first day when I realised there had been a mistake. Instead of Rachel, I was seated beside Nicola, a complete randomer. It turned out that somebody else from another primary school had the same initials and date of birth as me, so there had been a mix-up in our nominations. Annoyingly at the time, the school did nothing to rectify this, meaning I was stuck with Nicola while Rachel was stuck with some other girl who shared my birthday. But in the long run, it ended up being a blessing in disguise.

Rachel and I drifted apart as the school years went by mainly because she fell in with the wrong type of people whereas I grew closer to Nicola until we became bona fide best friends, which we still are to this day. I still have Rachel on my various social media channels, but we don't speak, and we certainly don't go for catch-ups on weekday evenings like Nicola and I like to do. It's funny how life works out in the end. Maybe it was fate that I met Nicola, just like how I met Tom. Or maybe it's all just a load of good and bad luck jumbled up together.

'I recommend the espresso martini,' Nicola says after we have spent a few quiet seconds browsing through the cocktail list.

'I like the sound of that,' I reply before we get the attention of the waitress who seated me, and give her our order.

As our drinks are being prepared, we waste no time getting down to business, or more specifically, my business.

'So, any news on the wedding?' Nicola asks me, wriggling in her seat with excitement, as if it was her partner who had proposed to her on a beach in Greece last month and not mine. Sadly for her, she is single, although she will be my maid of honour for the big day, tentatively scheduled for some time next summer if Tom and I can find a place to have it.

'We're seeing another couple of venues this week-end,' I reply, thinking ahead to the beautiful hotels I will be shown around in the coming days while Tom follows behind me, no doubt baulking at how much it might cost us. 'Slater's and Church Lane.'

'Very nice! Slater's is amazing. A girl in my office got married there. I only went to the evening do, but it was lovely.'

'It looks stunning. I just hope we can afford it.'

'Yeah, it's not cheap. What about Heron's Barn?'

I shake my head. 'I thought about it, but Rachel is the wedding planner there, so it might be a bit awkward.'

'Oh,' Nicola says, pulling her face, which makes me laugh because she always grimaces comically when I mention my 'ex-best friend'. 'How do you know?' she asks.

'She posts stuff all the time on Facebook about it. You know, things like *Come to our open day this weekend. Book your summer wedding now.* I think she's worked there for years.'

'That doesn't mean you can't get married there.'

'I know, but I just want to enjoy every part of this, and having someone I used to be close to organising my wedding might be a bit weird.'

'Fair enough,' Nicola says just before the waitress returns with our drinks.

'Cheers,' I say, raising my glass. 'Here's to hopefully finding the perfect venue this week.'

'Cheers,' Nicola replies, carefully touching her cocktail against mine so as not to spill any of the precious liquid.

'I still can't believe you're getting married,' Nicola says with a wry grin after we have taken a sip. 'Hearts will be breaking all over town when you walk down that aisle.'

'I doubt it,' I reply, chuckling at her comment.

'All the boyfriends you had?'

'I didn't have that many!'

'Are you kidding? I lost count at ten!'

'Oi, cheeky!' I say, playfully slapping Nicola's arm as she reaches for her drink again. 'Tom is only my sixth, I'll have you know. And my last.'

'I'm joking,' Nicola replies with that scampish grin of

hers. 'But I'm going to have some serious fun when I make my speech at your wedding.'

'You are not making a speech!'

'Why not? Because it's not tradition?'

'No. Because you know too much about me!'

We both laugh loudly, and it's enough to attract the attention of the couple sitting at the table nearest to us, who turn and give us a stern look. It seems to say that we are bringing down the ambience of this classy establishment, but it only makes us giggle even more.

After we have composed ourselves and taken another sip of our drinks, I move on to the next important topic of discussion.

'How's the planning for the hen do going?'

'Good, all the names you gave me are on board, so now I just need to pick a venue for it,' Nicola replies, seeming confident about the part of the wedding planning she is involved in. As my maid of honour, one of her many roles is to organise my hen do, which gives me heart palpitations if I think about it too much.

Before we know it, we have drained our first cocktail and are ready to order more, so I grab the menu and prepare to pick again. As I do, Nicola takes out her phone to check her messages, and that's how I find out about the body in the woods.

'Oh, my god, Shaun Gibson is dead,' Nicola says, staring at her phone screen with wide eyes.

'What?'

'He hanged himself!'

None of what my friend has just said to me makes any sense, so I hold out my hand for her phone, and she gives it to me, aware that if this is true, I need to know all the details. Sure enough, it seems she has got her facts right.

Shaun is dead. He was found hanging from a tree in

the woods just outside our hometown of Blackburn. It's all over Facebook. Old school friends are talking about it. Paying tribute. Expressing shock. Handling their grief. There are several old photos of Shaun in his school uniform posted, along with various love heart emojis and sad faces. But I don't need to see all these photos to remember what Shaun was like back then. I remember well enough.

That's because Shaun was my first boyfriend.

## 2

I was sixteen when I got my first boyfriend. At an age when I already had enough on my plate with GCSE exams, school-corridor gossip, and teenage hormones, I added another complicating factor to my life when I accepted Shaun Gibson's invitation to the bowling alley in the town centre.

It had been a rainy Friday night when I arrived at the venue for our first date, worrying about how the weather had wreaked havoc with my hair as well as how stupid my feet were going to look in the silly shoes that people have to wear when they go bowling. But it turned out I needn't have been so worried because from the first minute of the date until the last, Shaun did nothing but put me at ease with his jokes, his flirty banter, and his surprisingly caring attitude.

He bought me snacks from the café, and while it was nothing fancy, it still would have cost him a small fortune considering how little money sixteen-year-olds have at their disposal. He entered my name onto the screen before our game began, which was handy because I would never have been able to figure out how to do it myself. And he spent most of the night helping me try to knock down all the pins with the heavy bowling balls, offering me tips on how to throw, where to stand, and which ball was the best one to use for each scenario. He even asked for the side rails to be put up after he saw how bad I was, giving me a chance to at least get my ball to the end of the alley without it scuttling off harmlessly into the gutter.

Two hours went by in the blink of an eye before the date came to an end, with us both standing outside the bowling alley waiting for our parents to pick us up. I had been hoping he was going to kiss me before they arrived, and I wasn't disappointed. A couple of text messages between the two of us later that night confirmed it.

We were officially a couple.

Like all news tended to do in school, word got around quickly that Shaun and I were dating, not that we were exactly shy in showing our affection to each other. We would hold hands in the corridor. We would kiss by the side of the football fields. And we were pretty much inseparable for the rest of that final year, as well as the two years immediately after that in sixth form. Altogether, I was in a relationship with Shaun for two and a half years, which is a long time for anybody, never mind a couple of teenagers who naively thought that everything lasted forever, especially love.

Alas, it was not to be, and the curtain came down on our romance just two weeks shy of my nineteenth birthday. Both of us were at university at the time, me having started an economics degree in Sheffield, while he was up in Edinburgh learning how to be a dentist. Perhaps the writing had been on the wall for us before we had each left our hometown and set off in different directions, or maybe we really did have a chance of making it work long distance, but in the end, being apart proved too much for us. We were both in a new place, meeting new people and creating new memories, and our love that had been forged in the bowling alley, school corridors, and childhood bedrooms of Blackburn soon lost its shine as we moved into the world of nightclubs, pubs, and campus accommodation.

I was the one to bring the relationship to an end, phoning Shaun one blustery Tuesday evening as I walked through Sheffield city centre on my way to meet my uni mates for a pub quiz and another night out. It promised to be a good evening, but it was tainted by Shaun's reaction to my call, and the sound of him sobbing down the phone to me while begging me to reconsider was not a pleasant one. I felt terrible for making him so upset, even though I knew I was doing the right thing. I was only eighteen, but I'd already realised that not everybody is meant to fall in love at school and marry their childhood sweetheart. The world isn't as simple as that. Maybe that's how it is for some people, but I realised I wasn't one of them. There are billions of us, which means it's unlikely we will ever just be attracted to one person. I had enjoyed being in a relationship and calling myself somebody's girlfriend, but I also liked the idea of being free and single too, able to enjoy what life had in store for me without the risk of feeling guilty or as though I was being held back by something. I know Shaun didn't see it that way at first, but I'm sure he had much more fun at his university once we were no longer together.

I know I certainly did.

I didn't see Shaun after that for almost seven years. By then, we were both in our mid-twenties and in very different places in our lives. I had just come home to visit family and friends in between my travelling adventures, while he was much more settled as a qualified dentist working at a surgery in town. Our paths crossed randomly in one of the local pubs on a Saturday night, and an initially awkward interaction ended with us doing a shot of tequila together before wishing each other all the best.

Apart from that one 'catch-up', I hadn't seen Shaun again, and the only times I ever thought of him were when he posted something on his social media pages. I would occasionally like some of his updates or photos, although I tended to stay away from all the cheesy dentist memes that he shared from time to time. But from what I could tell, he seemed as if he was doing well. Besides his job, he had a partner and a young daughter, Lily, who I believe is about five or six. His current profile picture is an image of him and his daughter, both of them beaming widely into the camera on what looks like a fun family day out at the park.

But now Shaun is dead – and he took his own life.

Suicide. *I can't believe it.* I guess he wasn't as happy as his social media pictures suggested.

The news from Nicola hit me like a punch to the stomach, not because I still harboured any romantic feelings for my old flame but because of the shocking nature of it. Shaun is the same age as me. Thirty-six. Still so young. He should have been around for many years to come. But now he's gone, and he's left a partner and a young child behind who are no doubt going to miss him terribly. I'll miss him too, in a way, even though he wasn't a fixture in my daily life anymore. While he wasn't a part of my present or future, he was very much a part of my past.

My first date. My first kiss.

My first experience of love.

I lost my virginity to Shaun. It happened one night at

his mum and dad's house while they were out. We'd had popcorn and watched a movie downstairs before going up to his bedroom and going all the way. That momentous occasion in my life means it has always been impossible to forget about him.

I feel terrible for the fact that Shaun must have felt so low that he saw no other way out. Had he always harboured dark thoughts, or was it a recent thing? Did he contemplate suicide when I was with him? Could my sudden break-up with him at eighteen have had a lasting effect on his mental health?

It's impossible to know, but I can't think that way. It was eighteen years ago. Everybody had moved on. Whatever has been troubling him was surely something much more recent. But I'd leave it to the people online to speculate or point fingers of blame. No doubt there will be some who will do that in amongst all the touching tributes and happy photos. Both sides of social media, the good and the pure evil, will be in full view, I'm sure.

But there is no doubt that today is a sad day.

That might explain why I stayed out late with Nicola before eventually calling it a night and arriving home very late and very drunk.

Tom wasn't impressed when I eventually stumbled in.

I guess I've got some making up to do tomorrow.

## 3

I know that going out and getting drunk on a week night isn't the most sensible way for a woman my age to behave, so I can understand why Tom was a little peeved when I came crashing through the front door just after twelve last night. He was already in bed, like any conscientious employee who had to be up for work in six hours would be. But there was no chance of him being able to sleep, and not just because I turned on half the lights in the house and tripped over the washing basket in the downstairs hallway.

He wasn't able to get a good night's sleep because he couldn't relax until I was home, and he knew I was safe.

Bless him.

I've always told him that he shouldn't worry about me when I'm out with Nicola. It's not as if we're frequenting anywhere 'dodgy', and besides, I'm a big girl, I can look after myself. But of course, it's not as simple as that. He's my fiancé, which means worrying about me is just part of his life now. I'm the same with him when he goes out with his friends. No matter how well I know that he will be fine, it still doesn't stop me from being uneasy until I hear his key in the lock and feel assured that he has come back to me instead of ending up face down in a gutter somewhere after being attacked or getting run over by a car.

It should be more of a worry if he wasn't bothered by what I got up to, so I am grateful that I have a partner who cares about me. But that doesn't mean I haven't got some apologising to do for ruining his sleep and forcing him to go into his office today without a proper night's rest.

Fortunately, I know just the right thing to do to make it up to him. I've cooked his favourite meal, spaghetti bolognese with a generous helping of garlic bread on the side, and I'm sure it is just the thing he needs after a long day at work. But it's not really the thing I need after last night.

All I want to do now is crawl into bed and sleep off my headache.

'Something smells good,' Tom says as he enters the kitchen, looking extremely dashing in his shirt and tie.

'I should hope so. I've slaved over this for hours,' I say jokingly. In reality, I only got home from work half an hour before him, and it's not exactly the most taxing meal to cook for someone as experienced in the kitchen as I am.

He gives me a kiss before asking if he has time for a quick shower before it's ready, and I tell him that he does. With him out of the way again, I'm able to go into the cupboard above the microwave and take out another couple of pills to help with my banging head without him seeing me.

It's not that he wouldn't have some sympathy for me in my current state, but it would give him even more cause to try to get me to curtail my midweek jaunts with Nicola in favour of a much quieter evening at home with him in front of the TV. While he might have a point about me not being as young as I used to be, I definitely do not want to put a stop to my nights with my best friend, or any other friend for that matter.

I've always been a 'social butterfly', one of those people who enjoys the company of others and is easily able to network and mingle with all sorts of people, so having a busy social calendar is important to me. The problem is, when I socialise, I also like to drink, and that's where Tom has a point.

My body definitely takes longer to recover than it used to after a late night.

But as my headache continues to get worse even with the extra helping of pills I have just washed down, I start to fear that it isn't just a result of one too many cocktails last night.

It may also be the long-term effects of an accident I had when I was sixteen.

I had been in my final year of school, still a couple of months away from starting my relationship with Shaun, when I had woken up in a hospital bed with no memory of how I had got there. I was told by a doctor that I had been found unconscious in a park near my home by a member of the public who had called an ambulance, and apparently, I'd suffered what seemed like a heavy blow to the head. Fortunately, all the brain scans had come back clear for any signs of obvious damage, and I was hopeful that my full memory of the incident would return.

But it never has.

All I have been left with to remember that night twenty years ago is a scar on the back of my head that I can feel when I run my fingers through my hair and occasional migraines, although calling them that is doing them a serious disservice.

They feel more like somebody has attached a vice to my head and is steadily making it tighter.

I take a deep breath and try to distract myself from the numbing pain by finishing up the meal and serving it into two bowls. Then I grab the garlic bread and a couple of glasses of water, and now everything is ready to go.

'Dinner's ready!' I call up the stairs, and even the sound of my raised voice is like a drill to my fuzzy brain. All I want to do now is lie down in a dark room, but I need to get through this meal with Tom first. I'm trying to make it up to him after last night, so leaving him to eat on his own isn't really a part of the plan.

Tom eventually comes and joins me, his hair still wet from the shower and his shirt and tie replaced by an old T-shirt and a scruffy pair of jogging bottoms that I thought I'd hidden from him.

'Thanks, love,' he says to me as he takes a seat at the table and reaches for a slice of garlic bread.

Considering that I know he is in a mood with me after my late night, he still treats me very well, but that doesn't mean I can take him for granted. While Nicola might like to joke about how many boyfriends I have had, there is no doubt that Tom is the best of that bunch by a long way. He's funnier, smarter, and sexier than all those guys, not to mention a great cook in his own right, as well as being pretty handy when it comes to DIY duties. That's why I had no hesitation in saying yes to his marriage proposal. He is my perfect man, and I adore him.

I know he adores me too. He just wishes I wouldn't get so drunk in the middle of the week and trip over the stupid washing basket at midnight.

'How is it?' I ask as I watch him tucking in.

'Perfect as always,' he says, giving me the thumbs up. 'Just what I need after today.'

'Rough day at the office?'

'Yeah. You try sitting through high-pressure meetings with a bunch of lawyers on only a couple of hours' sleep.'

I grimace as he finishes his sentence. He's clearly still a little tetchy about last night.

'What kept you and Nicola out so late this time?' he asks me as he twirls another piece of spaghetti around his fork. 'I did ask you when you got in, but you were slurring your words so much, I gave up.'

I laugh, and even though Tom does his best not to do the same, he can't help it in the end.

'We had all the wedding stuff to go over,' I tell him, talking with a mouthful of garlic bread because now that we're engaged, I no longer have to try to impress him. 'I was telling her about the venues we are going to look at this weekend.'

'For five hours?'

'Well, that wasn't all we talked about,' I admit, although I'm not sure how honest I really want to be with him. The truth is that we spent much of the evening talking about Shaun after finding out that he had died. But I'm not sure telling Tom that I was out late discussing one of my exes is the best thing to do.

Or maybe I'm just being silly.

'There was some shocking news,' I say, deciding to just go for it. 'We found out one of the guys we used to go to school with hanged himself.'

'Gosh, really?'

I nod. 'Yeah, it's such a shame.'

'Did you know him well?'

'Kind of. But I hadn't seen him for a long time,' I say, leaving it at that.

'God, that's awful. Does he have a wife?'

'No. But he was seeing someone, and they had a daughter together.'

'That's terrible. Do they have any idea why he did it?'

'Nobody seems to know.'

We continue eating our meal in silence for a few moments, the heavy topic of conversation not conducive to more of a lively atmosphere. I wonder if Tom is feeling a little bad now about the fact that he was grumpy with me when I came home late, after learning that I got some sad news while I was out. But I also feel a little bad for not telling him the full story of why I ended up drinking so much last night: that I was so stunned that my first-ever boyfriend's life had ended in such a tragic manner.

I hate keeping things from Tom, so I'm just about to mention that I was romantically involved with the deceased many years ago when I get another surge of pain in my skull that almost makes my eyes water.

'Are you okay?' Tom asks, having spotted my discomfort.

'Not really. My head's banging.'

'I'm not surprised.'

'No, it's not that,' I assure him. 'It's the other kind of headache.'

Tom knows what I mean straight away because I've told him all about my accident when I was younger, or at least what I can remember of it, which is very little.

'Do you want me to get you anything?' he asks, the meal on his plate taking a back seat to the worry he has for my well-being.

'No, thank you. But I think I'm going to have to go and lie down.'

Tom understands, and he gives my hand a squeeze

for support as I walk past him, out of the kitchen in the direction of the staircase. I know this feeling will pass in an hour or two, and I'll be back to my old self then, but right now I feel incredibly fragile, and I need to be on my own.

It's a relief to get on the bed and close my eyes, and just as I predicted, the throbbing in my skull eases off the longer I lie in the dark.

I can hear my phone vibrating on the bedside table as I slowly feel myself coming back to full health, and by the time I reach out for it and pick it up, the clock on the screen tells me that I have been up here for almost an hour.

I'm just about to get off the bed and go down to see Tom again when I notice the message from Nicola.

*Shaun's funeral is on Friday at 2pm. Moorgate Chapel. Do you want to go?*

# 4

I s it wrong to go to an ex's funeral? Let's examine the evidence.

I feel guilty that I haven't told Tom, so that suggests it's a yes. I feel nervous about being here, which again hints that I made a mistake. And I feel as if I don't belong here, standing on the edge of so many grieving family members, which again tells me that I've done the wrong thing in coming to this event.

But I also feel sad for the man everybody is here for today. I can see the coffin at the front of the chapel and know that it contains Shaun, a person I used to love. More so, he used to love me too, so in that respect, maybe it would be strange if I weren't here.

I spent the last few days mulling over the decision of whether or not to be here ever since Nicola sent me that message with the details of the funeral. At first, I was a definite no, and I said as much in my reply to her. It simply felt too strange to think about saying my good-byes to a man I dated eighteen years ago but have only seen once since. But Nicola's reply got me thinking. She told me that she assumed I would want to go, having been so close to the deceased. She also said something that made me feel a little guilty.

She said that she believed Shaun would have attended my funeral if the situation had been reversed.

That got me thinking, and it wasn't the only thing. In the days after the discovery of Shaun's body, the time-lines of my social media accounts were flooded with posts from old school acquaintances who were all discussing the tragic news as well as campaigning for a big show of support for Shaun's family at the funeral. Maybe it would have been different if the circumstances surrounding his death were altered, but the fact it was suicide seemed to make everybody determined to show how much Shaun was really loved.

It seemed like everyone in our school year was going, and Nicola told me as much, saying that she was going to attend to offer her support too. But I was still conflicted, aware that I would have to mention it to Tom and assuming he might find it strange that I wished to go to the funeral of an old partner.

I tried to put myself in his shoes and imagine what I would feel like if he told me he was going to the funeral of one of his exes. Would I feel uncomfortable, or would I understand? But my imagination has never been great, even before I suffered the mysterious head injury at sixteen, so I found it impossible to predict how he would react. That might explain why I still haven't told him.

In the end, my decision was made based on something I read online. I'd resorted to good old Google to help make the decision for me, typing in 'Would you go to an ex's funeral?' and seeing what the wisdom of the internet had to offer me. I had expected the majority of answers to confirm what I already suspected, which was that it would be weird, awkward, and unnecessary, considering we hadn't been close for such a long time. But to my surprise, many of the search results suggested that it would be a nice gesture if I attended. They said that an ex is a big part of anybody's life, so why not acknowledge it? I had to agree with that. Shaun had certainly been a big part of my teenage years. But it was the numerous comments I saw on message boards and forums debating the topic that really gave me my decision. Several people had wisely observed that people don't usually regret the things they do, but rather the things they didn't do. The implication was that in time, I would regret it more if I didn't go than if I did.

With that in mind, I had sent another message to Nicola, telling her that I would attend the funeral with her.

And now, here I am.

Moorgate Chapel is a small building tucked away at the end of a leafy lane, and it would look quite pretty in another setting. But with this being Blackburn, a northern town not far from the desolate West Pennine Moors, the weather doesn't usually lend itself to people being outdoors and enjoying the view. Today is no different, and I barely had time to look where I was going as I ran from the taxi into the chapel, doing my best not to take a beating from the howling wind and the driving rain that has tormented this part of the world almost every day for as long as I can remember.

Due to the inclement weather, the chapel floor is now soaking wet thanks to all the water brought in on the bottoms of the shoes of the mourners, and the whole place has that awful smell of damp that comes on a rainy day. Maybe that's why I'm feeling particularly glum as I stand to the right-hand side of the entrance by myself, feeling awkward and generally trying to avoid making eye contact with anyone until Nicola turns up.

Or maybe it's just because of the sad sights I have seen since I arrived here ten minutes ago.

The rumours on social media were right. Shaun's old classmates have come out in force, and the chapel is now a sea of black as more and more mourners file inside, dressed appropriately for such a sombre occasion. I've seen a few faces I recognise from school, although not well enough for me to go over to say hello, but it was the sight of two people I used to know very well that reminded me how tragic this day really is. Shaun's parents had passed through the large entrance and made their way past the rows of pews, their faces displaying how grief-stricken they were, and their bodies hunched and stiff, as if they had aged a hundred years overnight. But I know that they are still a relatively young couple, only in their mid-fifties, and like most parents, they surely never imagined the day when they would have to bury their child.

I know their names are Bryan and Janet, as well as the fact that he has a wicked sense of humour while she can make a mean casserole, because I spent numerous hours round at their house when I was dating their son. Barbecues on a Saturday in the garden. Roast dinners around the kitchen table on a Sunday. And countless nights in front of the TV in their lounge, Shaun and I cuddled up on one sofa while they were snuggled up on their own.

His parents always treated me well and welcomed me into their family, even though they must have known that at our age, there was a good chance the romance wasn't going to last forever. After my break-up with Shaun, I often wondered what his parents had said about me and the way I had ended things with him.

Did they hate me? Did they call me a cold-hearted bitch? Or did they simply console their son, aware that break-ups were unfortunately just a part of life for many people, and nobody had to be the bad guy?

I obviously never knew the answer, but having watched them reach the front of the chapel and slowly take their seats today, my heart broke for them and what they had lost.

But the most arresting sight had come a few moments later, when Shaun's partner and their daughter had entered the chapel, the mother's pain evident as she sobbed while gripping the hand of her child and navigating her way through the crowded entrance. I noticed how confused the young girl looked as she stared up at all the strange faces, each of whom offered a warm smile back to her as she moved amongst them in a flowing black dress.

I kept my eyes on Shaun's partner as she reached the front and received a hug from Bryan before the father of the deceased knelt down and spoke with his little grandchild. Tears pricked at my eyes the longer I watched them, and even though I knew it would be healthier for me to look away, I found it impossible to do so. I also felt guilty that I had been needlessly ruminating over my decision of whether to attend today, while those poor people had been going through the worst time of their lives.

Fortunately, Nicola arrived a moment later, providing me with a much-needed distraction, and we quickly took a seat on the back row to get out of the way of the other mourners, who I still felt had more of a right to be here than I did.

By the time the doors to the chapel were closed, everybody was in their seats, and nobody was speaking. There simply wasn't much to say then.

The coffin at the front said it all.

---

## 5

The funeral service was short, difficult, and filled with the sounds of sobbing, as most of these services tend to be. In the end, it had been a relief to get out of that chapel and back into the fresh air, even if the rain had still been coming down in bucket-loads. At least outside, I hadn't had to look at that coffin any longer, nor had I been so confronted with the pained expressions of Shaun's family and closest friends, all of whom had eventually departed from a different exit in preparation for the burial.

Perhaps I should have gone home at that point. I'd done what I'd set out to do and paid my respects. I should have called it a day. But then Nicola had persuaded me to come for one drink at the wake. It might have been the fact that the rain was lashing down onto me while she had a taxi already waiting that convinced me to go with her, but here I am now, standing by the bar, with a free glass of wine in my hand. The buffet is laid out on the tables across the room, and the tab behind the bar is said to be a generous one, so all the mourners currently in this pub are not in any danger of going without refreshments.

At first, I wondered how much Bryan and Janet must have spent on all of this. After all, with at least eighty people at the funeral, there was bound to be plenty of demand for the drinks they had paid for. But then I overheard somebody in the buffet queue mention that the landlord of this pub was covering the costs himself, having known Shaun since he was a young boy and feeling like he wanted to do something kind for the grieving family. It's an impressive gesture, and while it won't do anything to bring Shaun back, I have no doubt it has made things just a little bit easier for his parents. Lord knows they deserve it.

I take another sip of my wine as I spot Nicola making her way back from the toilets at the other end of the bar, and I'm just about to tell her that I'm ready to leave when I hear a female voice behind me.

'Adele Davies! I thought it was you!'

I turn around, having no idea who the mystery speaker could be until I lay eyes on her, and I know instantly. It's Rachel. Great. If I wasn't feeling awkward enough being at my ex's funeral, now I've just been accosted by my ex-best friend.

'Rachel, oh my gosh. How are you?'

We hug awkwardly before separating.

'How many years has it been?' she asks me, even though we both know the answer.

We haven't been best friends for twenty-five years, and we haven't seen each other in person for twenty.

'I can't remember, but it's been a while,' I reply, hoping that's a convincing response.

'How have you been? You look well!'

'I'm good, actually. How are you?'

I wonder how long this cringe-fest of a conversation

must go on, but it seems it will be a little while yet because Rachel quickly notices the ring on my finger.

'What is that?' she cries, grabbing my hand for a closer look.

'Oh, yeah. Erm, I'm engaged now.'

'I thought I saw something on Facebook! Well, lucky you, that's quite a rock you have there!'

I laugh while doing my best to downplay it. I know Tom spent a fortune on it, but I'm not a flashy person at all and don't actually like all the extra attention it gets me. I told him I'd be happy with a Haribo ring on as long as I got to marry him, and while that was a joke, he had exceeded my expectations when it came to this piece of jewellery.

'When's the big day?' Rachel asks, still ogling the ring.

'Oh, we haven't set a date yet. It'll be sometime next summer.'

'Well, I'm sure it'll be amazing whenever it happens.'

I smile as she finally lets go of my hand, while feeling extremely awkward that she won't be invited. As if this exchange couldn't get any more uncomfortable, my current best friend arrives right on cue to enter the fray.

'Hi, Rachel, isn't it?' Nicola asks, offering her best fake smile to the woman who was once her biggest rival for my friendship.

'Yes, that's right. Sorry, have we met?'

I grimace slightly at Rachel's display of confusion. There's no doubt she knows who Nicola is, but I guess she is just playing a game. She played a lot of them when we were younger.

'Once or twice,' Nicola replies graciously. 'Terribly sad day, isn't it?'

'It is,' Rachel says, before thankfully deciding that

the conversation might be less awkward elsewhere. 'Well, it was nice to see you, Adele. And good luck for the big day.'

I smile as Rachel hurries away in the direction of the buffet before catching the look on Nicola's face and trying not to laugh.

'Did you see that? She pretended she didn't know who I was!' Nicola cries, a little too loudly for the mood in the room, so I tell her to hush.

'Forget about it. She was just being funny.'

'I guess she's still annoyed about how things ended up between you two.'

'I doubt that. She's got plenty of friends now,' I say, watching Rachel chatting away with a couple of other women I recognise from our school year. Unlike me, it looks like she has made more of an effort to keep in touch with some of these people since we left.

'Oh, I got you another glass of wine, by the way,' Nicola says, suddenly thrusting a fresh glass into my hand.

'I was going to leave after this one!'

'We're here to remember Shaun,' Nicola reminds me somewhat seriously before adding, 'And it's a free bar, so drink up.'

I smile as I finish my first glass, and I'm just about to take a sip of my second when I hear the loud call of the man in the doorway across the room.

'Sorry to interrupt, guys, but Shaun's family have really been touched today to see so many of his school friends come to pay their respects. They have asked if we could all gather outside the pub for a photo, so if you'd like to be in it, please make your way outside now. Thanks.'

The request came from Gareth, Shaun's best friend from school. He had made a poignant and touching speech at the funeral, which had left most of the mourners, including me, in tears.

No sooner has he finished speaking than I see many of the people in the room start to make their way outside in anticipation of the photo. But I'm not so sure.

'People don't usually take pictures at funerals, do they?' I ask Nicola, who, like me, hasn't joined the rest of our classmates in heading for the door.

'No, it's a bit weird,' she replies. 'But I guess it's something for his family to look back on and see how many people Shaun had in his life.'

'What should we do?'

'I guess we'd better go outside.'

I leave my glass of wine on the bar beside Nicola's before following her out of the pub and into the last dregs of daylight beneath an overcast sky. At least it has stopped raining now.

Gareth tells everybody where to stand, and Nicola and I do our best to squeeze onto the end of the large group huddled in front of the pub as some old chap in a black suit prepares to take our photo on a mobile phone. I assume that we're not supposed to smile for this, but I don't want to look too sad either, so I do my best to keep a blank expression on my face as the picture is taken.

'That's great. Thanks, guys,' Gareth says as the group starts to break up. 'Just something for the family to look back on when they feel ready to.'

Nicola was right. The photo was for Shaun's family, and as we make our way back inside, I'm glad I was a part of it. I also wonder if his parents will notice me standing on the end and recognise me as their son's first girlfriend. Perhaps, but that's okay. I'm sure they will be glad I came to pay my respects. And I'm glad I came too.

The strangers on the internet were right.

You will regret the things you didn't do more than the things you did.

## 6

Maybe I spoke too soon. I might have been wrong, just like all those people on the internet.

I do regret something I did.

I regret having several glasses of wine at the wake today.

I know I'm drunk because I've dropped my front door keys twice since I got out of the taxi, and I'm not even halfway up my driveway yet. I also know I'm drunk because I keep trying not to laugh as I attempt to pick them up, aware that I must look ridiculous to the driver, who is still parked outside my house. But finally, I get my keys off the concrete and jab them into the door, turning the lock and stumbling inside as the car drives away.

That's one tricky task dealt with.

Now it's time for another.

'There you are! I've been worried sick!' Tom cries as he rushes through the hallway towards me. 'Where the hell have you been?'

I put my entire bodyweight into the front door as I

close it, not because I need the extra strength, but I do need the support. I feel like I could fall over, and somehow, I don't think that will go down too well with my concerned fiancé.

'I'm sorry. My battery died,' I explain, though I know it's not much of an excuse to not tell my partner where I've been for the last several hours.

The wake started out quiet and polite, like all wakes do, before gradually getting rowdier and more celebratory as the alcohol kicked in and everybody took full advantage of the free bar after a day of staring death in the face. Nicola and I had been no exception, and we had found ourselves going back to the bar with increasing regularity as the hours slipped by and our inhibitions lowered. What had begun as an awkward occasion for me had eventually turned into a great opportunity to catch up with old faces from my past. It hadn't taken long for me to start mingling around the pub, and I had even ended up having another chat with Rachel, although the second one had been much better than the first.

While the confidence boost from the alcohol had made me feel even better about my decision to go to the funeral, it had undoubtedly made things worse for me the later I stayed. I hadn't told Tom where I was, assuming I'd easily be home before him, and he'd never have to know. But that idea is almost laughable now considering it's gone ten, and I've only just made it back. Not only that but my phone died around seven, so I've been off the grid for the last three hours, which explains why Tom is looking at me like I'm a terrible fiancée, which I guess I am, at least tonight anyway.

'Were you out with Nicola again?' he asks me, shaking his head as he observes my battle to stay upright by the front door.

'Yeah,' I reply, although I'm aware it comes out as more of a 'yerrrr', as my tongue struggles to keep up with what my brain is trying to make it do.

'There's a shock. Couldn't you have messaged me off her phone to let me know what you were up to? Anything so I haven't been sitting here wondering if you're lying dead in a ditch somewhere.'

'Don't be silly,' I say, with what is no doubt a very silly grin on my face. 'I'm fine.'

'You don't look it. You can barely stand!'

Those words from Tom are a reminder that I'm not doing as good a job of getting upstairs to bed as I would have hoped, so I take a deep breath and push myself away from the door in an attempt to close the gap between me and the mattress.

But it's a mistake, and while the top half of my body is ready to move, the bottom is struggling to keep up, meaning I fall forward and land on the carpet with a thud before bursting out laughing and pawing at Tom's feet.

'Jesus, Adele, you're thirty-six. When are you two going to grow up?'

I run my hand down his jeans, feeling the texture of the denim and wondering who invented it and why it feels so good.

'I'm sorry. Can you help me up?' I ask, even though I'm tempted just to curl up on this carpet and get some sleep here.

'Come on,' Tom says, putting his hands beneath my arms and lifting me back to my unsteady feet. 'Let's get you to bed.'

He leads me to the staircase, and what should be a ten-second job ends up taking more like two minutes before he is able to get me all the way up.

'You're the best,' I tell him as he leads me into the

bedroom, but he says nothing as I flop down onto the bed and make a strange noise as I try to figure out what is happening with the duvet and why I'm not under it already.

It takes me a while to realise that it's because I'm lying on top of it.

After more help getting into bed from my perfect partner, as well as using his assistance in plugging my phone into the charger on the bedside table, I'm finally tucked in and resting with my head on my pillow, although now that I am, I suddenly feel too wired to think about sleep.

I want to chat, and poor Tom is going to have to humour me.

'Tell me about your night,' I say as if I'm in any fit state to hold a sensible conversation.

'How about you tell me where you've been,' Tom replies, taking a seat on the bed beside me. 'Where did Nicola take you this time? A nightclub? A bar full of twenty-year-olds?'

I know Tom disapproves of Nicola and how often she has me out with her, and I also know this isn't the right time to be honest about where I have been today, but screw it. I'm drunk, and I'm feeling good.

'I was at a funeral, actually,' I say, stifling a burp that could have easily turned into something much worse if the burning sensation of stomach acid in my throat is anything to go by. 'That guy from school. Remember, I told you about him.'

'The guy who hanged himself?'

'Yeah. It was his funeral today, and it was very sad, but there were so many people there, which was nice, don't you think?'

I stop talking because I can feel another burp coming on, and I don't want Tom to have something else to be disgusted by this evening. I think needing to be helped into bed is enough for one night.

'You told me you hadn't seen him for years,' Tom says.

'I hadn't. But loads of people from school were going, and Nicola went too, so I thought it would be nice to go.'

'And get hammered?'

'I was only planning on having one drink.'

'Looks like it went well,' Tom says, getting up off the bed and heading for the door.

'I'm sorry, babe,' I tell him before he can leave. 'Come to bed!'

'I'll be up soon,' he says as he leaves the room, and I'm not sure whether he is mad at me or not, but my brain is too fuzzy to try to work that out right now.

Instead, I sink deeper into my pillow, but before I drift off, I find the energy to fish my mobile phone out of my pocket and go onto social media. Almost instantly, I see the photo that was taken outside the pub, featuring the large group of Shaun's old school friends.

My eyes scan the various faces before I find myself. There I am, standing on the end beside Nicola, with my poker face on display. The plan was to not look too happy or too sad, and I seem to have done a pretty good job of it in the end. I've certainly done a better job of it than Nicola, who has a big grin on her face, which looks completely out of place for a funeral, although I do know that she was already a couple of glasses of wine ahead of me at that point, so maybe that explains it.

My thumb scrolls down the screen, and I see several more photos from the day, but I'm just about to close my eyes and finish looking at them tomorrow when I see the status update from one of my old university friends.

*Terribly sad news. I've just found out that Calum Jenkins*

*has died in a car accident. Gutted. Was looking forward to seeing him at the reunion next week. Thoughts with his family and friends. RIP, mate.*

The phone falls from my hand and bounces across the carpet away from the bed, but I didn't drop it because of how drunk I am. I dropped it because of the shock of the status update.

It seems I haven't just lost one ex-boyfriend this week.

I've now lost two.

## 7

I was twenty years old and in my final year at university when I started dating Calum Jenkins. After the break-up with Shaun and spending most of the two years that followed it living a carefree life on campus, it was a nice change of pace to find myself back in a relationship again. I had certainly not intended to become so involved with somebody in my last year in Sheffield, already having one eye on graduation and all the adventures that waited for me in the world after that. But even though I was young, I was already learning fast that when it comes to things like love, you can't plan for them. One day you just meet somebody, and the next you can't stop thinking about them.

That's how it was with Calum. We met on a Thursday night two weeks before Christmas, which can be a wild and debauched time of year for anyone, but even more so for students. I was out that night with my housemates, dressed as one of Santa's elves, when I bumped into a guy at the bar and spilt my drink all over his Christmas jumper. It had been a simple accident, but I felt guilty about the spillage, particularly because his jumper was one of those with flashing lights, and I worried that the liquid was going to short-circuit the battery and ruin Christmas for him forever. He told me not to worry about it and even offered to replace the drink I had lost during our collision, which was kind and also very helpful. I was a poor student, after all, and I'd pretty much blown through my budget for that term already.

It was while we were waiting to get served by one of the busy bar staff that we got to know each other a little better, passing comment on the state of the music in the bar, the state of our terrible outfits and the state of life as a student in general. By the time I had a fresh drink in my hand, I'd decided that I didn't want our interaction to end there, so I boldly told Calum to get his friends and come join my group over by the dance floor. He eagerly did as he was told, and it wasn't long until the two of us had locked lips on that dance floor, beginning a relationship that would go on to last for ten months.

Unfortunately, I had to take on the role of bad guy for the second time, as it was I who ultimately ended that romance too.

My reasons this time weren't too dissimilar from why I'd ended things with Shaun and boiled down to the fact that I didn't want to be in a long-distance relationship. Calum and I had been great together when we were both in Sheffield, but things became trickier after we had graduated and gone back to our respective hometowns. With me in Blackburn and him all the way across the country in 'Sunny Scunthorpe', my feelings for him started to fade not only because I no longer saw him every day, but because we had very different plans of how we wanted to spend the next chapter of our lives.

He was eager to enter the working world and put

down some roots, demonstrating a level of maturity I hadn't seen at all during his student days. But talking about finding a serious job was one thing. Talking about finding a house to rent together was another. Unlike him, I was nowhere near ready for anything that even remotely resembled 'settling down.' Instead, I had my heart set on one thing and one thing only.

Travelling.

I'd always known that I wanted to hit the open road as soon as I was free of education and before I had to conform to society's expectations and get myself a proper job. With my mind filled with visions of all sorts of exciting places like Brazil, Bali, and Bangkok, I couldn't even begin to entertain the idea of joining Calum in finding somewhere for us both to rent in Scunthorpe. Bless him, he did offer to move to Blackburn and leave behind his family and friends to make a real go of things with me, but even then, my hometown held little appeal for me when compared to all the unexplored cities and beaches of the world.

I told Calum that he should come with me, and it would be an adventure we could enjoy together, but it was obvious that he hadn't been bitten by the travelling bug and preferred to stay in England. He suggested we stay together to see how things went, but I already knew how that would end, and I didn't wish to spend half of my time abroad pining for somebody back home. That was why I made the difficult decision to bring an end to my second relationship, telling Calum the bad news one blustery Sunday afternoon as we walked along a street in his hometown.

Unlike with Shaun, when I hadn't been able to see the hurt on his face after I ended things over the phone, this time there was no way of avoiding how upset my ex was at the news. But after an awkward couple of minutes, Calum and I hugged and ended things on good terms before I left and boarded a train back to Blackburn, though really, I was destined for much more exotic climes soon after.

Because my relationship with Calum had come at a time when social media was just starting to become a thing, there had been only a couple of photos of the two of us online on my various accounts, which I eventually deleted, although I waited a while in case Calum was checking and it made him feel bad. That was back in 2006, and I never saw him again in person, although thanks to the explosion of social media around that time, I was able to see what he was up to every now and again through his various posts. It turned out that he got a new girlfriend not long after me, and they married three years later, while I was still very much living a nomadic lifestyle. But I was glad he was happy because he was a great guy, so it had seemed a shame when his marriage had come to an end a couple of years ago. I hadn't noticed too much of a presence from him online since then, but that is not unusual for my generation as we grow older and become less inclined to put every-thing that we do on the internet for people to look at.

I had probably gone two years without thinking about him until I saw the status saying that he had died in a car accident. Just like Shaun, another blast from my past. And just like him, another tragic death.

A car crash is a dramatic and brutal way to leave this world, and while I'm sure I will learn the details of the accident in time, that doesn't change the fact that it's a horrible and senseless way for a person to die. An inci-dent like this always makes me wonder about fate and if it was destined to happen. Was he just in the wrong place at the wrong time? Was it always going to happen, or would things have turned out differently if he'd made alternative choices in his life?

Would he still be alive if I had never broken up with him?

The silly thoughts are back again, just like they were after Shaun died, and even though I know this has nothing to do with me, that doesn't stop my stupid brain from creating these nonsensical notions that like to run away with themselves. But maybe I'm just being hard on myself. After all, I have just experienced two of my ex-boyfriends dying within days of each other. That is pretty random, and I'm having a hard time processing it. They're two men who had never met and were living very different lives before dying in very different ways. There is no link between either of them other than the one I'm aware of, which is that they were the first two men I ever dated. But that doesn't mean anything.

It's just an unfortunate coincidence.

Isn't it?

---

## 8

My head hurts. I definitely overdid it at the wake. But I'm not expecting to get much sympathy from Tom today after I neglected to let him know where I was.

The sound of the Hoover out in the hallway tells me that.

Dragging my weary body out of bed, I head for the bedroom door with one hand on my throbbing head, unable to hold off visiting the bathroom any longer. I know opening this door is going to subject me to the loud noises of the Hoover even more, but I can't help it, nor can I put off seeing Tom any longer.

I didn't hear him come to bed last night, although that's no great surprise considering I was dead to the world after drinking so much. But I didn't even hear him get up this morning either, instead just waking up alone in the bed, much like how I had been when I had fallen asleep. If it hadn't been for the Hoover, I wouldn't have known if he was still in the house, but he's definitely here all right.

My pounding head is all too aware of that.

Opening the bedroom door and peering out, I see Tom with his back to me, moving the Hoover over the carpet and seemingly unaffected by how disturbingly loud the tools of his work are. I creep out of the bedroom and think about just ducking into the bathroom without letting him know that I'm up, but in the end, I decide to stop pussyfooting around and just get it over with. If he's mad at me for last night, I'd rather have the argument now and be done with it.

Tapping my fiancé lightly on the shoulder, I do my best not to startle him, but it doesn't work, and he almost jumps out of his skin at my touch.

That's the problem with hoovering. You can't hear somebody creeping up behind you.

Fortunately, the shock wasn't severe enough to give him a heart attack, and he's able to turn off the Hoover before getting a good look at me and seeing just how much of a bad way I'm really in.

His facial expression says it all.

I must look terrible.

'She's alive,' Tom says sarcastically, with the hint of a smile that gives me hope that he isn't mad after all.

'I don't feel it,' I tell him, rubbing one of my bleary eyes while wishing that I could swap skulls with somebody else right now. Even with the Hoover off, I can still barely hear myself think. But it's hard to tell if it's just a headache caused by yesterday's events or another migraine from my old accident.

'There's some sausages and bacon in the fridge. What do you say I make you up a couple of sandwiches and a strong coffee to help get you through the morning?'

Tom's suggestion is a godsend and just what I need.

'What would I do without you?'

'I dread to think.'

I laugh and give him a kiss before heading into the bathroom, relieved that there doesn't seem to be any lasting damage from my performance last night. But that doesn't mean that I can keep behaving like this. He is right. I do need to dial it down a bit now that I'm getting older, as well as stop being so selfish. It was okay for me to go out drinking and not let anybody know where I was when I was younger, but now that I have a fiancé, I need to think of him too. I also need to consider my health. These drinking sessions with Nicola are doing nothing for my complexion or my insides, which are churning as I flush the toilet.

By the time I make it downstairs to the kitchen, the smell of bacon fills the air, as well as the sizzle of several sausages in the pan, and it's the light at the end of the tunnel I need to let me know that I'm going to survive this hangover like I survived all the others. It also helps that it's a Saturday. If this were a weekday, I'd probably be kissing my job goodbye.

'So, any gossip from the funeral, then?' Tom asks me as he turns over a couple of rashers of bacon.

'I wish I could remember,' I reply as I reach tentatively for the cup of coffee that was already waiting for me when I came down. It would be good to tell Tom more about the people I was with and the conversations I had yesterday even though he doesn't know any of the people: he went to a different school than I did. But I can barely remember getting home, never mind what I talked about in that pub.

'I've seen you've been getting tagged in plenty of photos,' he says as he slides two slices of bread into the toaster.

'Have I?'

I realise I've left my phone in the bedroom, but I

need food before I can even think about tackling the staircase again.

'Yeah. There's quite a few. I saw one of you and Shaun in your school days that somebody put up. You two looked close.'

The way he says that tells me that he has deduced that Shaun wasn't just some guy I went to school with. Maybe it's time for me to be completely transparent.

'I guess I should have told you that we used to date each other,' I say, regretting that I didn't just mention it the first time Shaun's name came up.

'Yeah, I figured that from all the photos of the two of you together. How long were you a couple?'

I'm wondering just how many photos have been posted online now, and I really want to go and get my phone, but I'd better field Tom's questions first.

'Two years. We broke up when I started uni.'

'And there was me thinking I knew all about your exes.'

'You do,' I reply with a chuckle, trying to keep it light. 'Mostly.'

'Is that why you didn't tell me the full story?'

'Kind of. I didn't know if you would feel weird about me going to an ex's funeral.'

'I don't feel weird about it,' Tom replies, although I'm not quite sure if he means it because his back is turned to me as he continues to cook.

'But seriously, I really only went because everyone from school was going.'

'Sure,' Tom says, but again it's in a way that offers me little indication of how he actually feels.

As he plates up the food and brings it over to the table, I wonder if I did make a mistake in going to the funeral. I can see why Tom might not have liked the idea of me doing something that involved an ex-partner.

He is my future, so why should I be concerning myself with my past? Then again, maybe this is more his problem than mine. I know that he has not had anywhere near as many relationships as I have had, and from what he has told me, I'm only his second serious partner. It's not that he's led a sheltered life, although, in comparison to me, I guess he has. Maybe that explains why I do my best not to bring up any of my exes if I can help it. I don't think that he's jealous, but I don't want to make him feel like I'm rubbing it in when I talk about all the guys who came before him.

That's why I'm not going to mention the news about Calum and the fact that he is the second ex-boyfriend of mine to die this week. There's no need, and I really hope nobody tags me in any photos like they have obviously been doing with Shaun. I'm not going to go to Calum's funeral – I don't feel the need to, and there's a big uni reunion next week, where I'll see all the same people in what will be a much lighter atmosphere.

I'm done with chapels, black dresses, and sombre speeches for a long time.

But as I tuck into my breakfast, I can't shake off that feeling of dread that seems to have been hanging over me ever since I saw the news of Calum's death on my phone last night. I know that hangovers are known to cause such feelings, so it's hard to tell if my current mood is just down to how much I had to drink yesterday or whether there is something genuine to worry about. But of course there isn't, and the more bacon and sausage I eat, the better I feel.

## 9

It's not just hangovers that get worse with age. It's the body's ability to perform simple exercises too. Quite why I thought getting a membership to my local gym was a good idea is beyond me, but like many things in my life, it started out as Nicola's idea. She's on the treadmill beside me, running just as fast as I am, yet I seem to be the only one struggling for breath. She wasn't always fitter than me, but she's definitely overtaken me when it comes to physical performance these days.

'I'm going to have to stop,' I say in between my desperate gasps of breath. 'I can't do it.'

'Just two more minutes! Keep going!' Nicola cries, her face a picture of determination, and I'm not sure if she's being my best friend or my personal trainer right now, but either way, I'm done.

I hit the red button in front of me, and the conveyor belt beneath my feet mercifully comes to a sudden stop.

That's better.

I don't feel like I'm dying anymore.

As I wait for Nicola to finish her run, I take a look

around the gym, but it's pretty quiet. It is Saturday afternoon, and most sensible people are spending their precious weekend elsewhere, shopping, drinking or putting their feet up and making the most of some freedom. But not me. I was stupid enough to think that a workout was the best way to spend my Saturday.

My eagerness to exercise today was because I was hoping the rush of endorphins that usually comes from such a healthy pursuit might help counteract the waves of paranoia I have been battling. Ever since I found out about Calum's death so soon after Shaun's, I haven't been able to shake the feeling that something is wrong, even though I know that I'm just being silly. Their deaths are not suspicious. There is nothing to suggest they are linked. And it's not as if any of my other exes have come to harm.

I need to stop worrying about it.

So why can't I?

As Nicola finally finishes her run and takes a swig from her water bottle, I decide to run the events of the past few days by her. I haven't mentioned Calum's death to her yet, but it's time to see if she thinks the timing of it is weird too.

'I got some more sad news the other day,' I say as we both step off our treadmills and make our way across the gym in the direction of the changing rooms. 'I found out Calum died. You remember, my boyfriend at uni?'

'Oh my gosh, I remember him! What happened?'

'He crashed his car. From the news articles online, it sounds like he went off the road.'

'God, that's awful. Was anybody else hurt?'

'No, just him.'

'Wow, poor guy. He was a good laugh, wasn't he?'

I nod my head as I think back on the man he used to be. Nicola met Calum a couple of times when she visited me at uni, and she got on well with him, as she often did with all my boyfriends. I could always tell the guys whom I dated were nervous when I introduced her to them because they knew that it was important to get the seal of approval from my best friend. But everybody passed with flying colours when it came to that. Well, almost everybody. My last boyfriend before I met Tom was a different story, but then again, it wasn't just Nicola who disapproved of him.

Everyone in my life did.

'That's two of my ex-boyfriends who have died in the same week,' I say, using my arm to wipe sweat from my forehead. 'What are the chances of that?'

'That is weird,' Nicola replies as she pauses to fill her water bottle up from the tap.

'That's what I thought.'

'Are you going to go to his funeral?'

'No. I think saying goodbye to one ex is enough for one week. Plus, Tom wasn't too thrilled when he found out I went to Shaun's.'

'Ouch. Did you two argue?'

'Not really. Tom's not like that. He just gets a bit grumpy and makes a few disparaging comments.'

'That's okay, then.'

'Yeah, but I'd rather not risk annoying him again by bringing up another ex's funeral.'

'It's sweet that he gets jealous. It shows how much he loves you.'

'He's not jealous. At least I don't think he is.'

'Babe, it's normal for people to be jealous of their partner's exes. You must feel like that about his.'

'He doesn't have that many.'

'But you've snooped online at the ones he does have, right?'

I laugh – I can't deny that. 'Maybe,' I admit.

'See. It's normal for him to feel weird when you bring up an ex-lover. But he should know he's got nothing to worry about, especially if they all keep dropping dead.'

'That's not funny,' I say, slapping my friend playfully on the arm as we move past the rows of exercise benches that are filled with the gym's most muscular clients, all of whom are curling weights in front of the wall of mirrors. That's where I also notice the man sitting on the exercise bench at the end, looking right back at me, or should I say staring right back at me.

'Oh no, Peter the Pervert is in again,' I say, nudging Nicola so that she can see him too.

That's the nickname the two of us have given to the creepy guy who always seems to just be sitting and ogling the female gym goers whenever we notice him here. I don't think I've ever seen him lift a weight or step on a treadmill, but I've certainly seen him watching me work out plenty of times before.

'He looks busy as always,' Nicola replies, and we laugh before heading into the changing rooms, where, thankfully, we are now out of view of Mr Pervert on the gym floor.

As I open my locker and pull out my bag of fresh clothes, I'm feeling better for getting out of the house and forcing myself to complete some exercise, even if I could definitely have done more. I'm also feeling better for having Nicola confirm that it is strange for two of my ex-boyfriends to pass away so closely together. I guess I'll just have to wait for the uneasy feeling I have to fade away, which it undoubtedly will once my social media timelines return to normal and I no longer keep seeing 'RIP' posts every time I go online.

'What have you got planned next weekend?' Nicola asks me as she peels off her sweaty T-shirt and tosses it into her locker, and I already know where she is going with that question. She'll be hoping that I'm free so she can pick out another bar for us to frequent at some point. But I'm afraid I'm going to have to disappoint her.

'I've got my uni reunion next Saturday,' I say, taking off my own T-shirt, although I seem to feel more self-conscious about doing so than Nicola ever does. The rest of the women in these changing rooms are always so toned and tanned, whereas I look very much like a typical Lancashire girl. Pale and a little squishy around the edges.

'Oh. Any chance I can come?'

'Not really. You need an invite.'

'You can sneak me in, can't you?'

'Are you kidding? I couldn't sneak you in anywhere. You're too loud for that.'

Nicola laughs and gives me a whack with one of her socks, and while I'm joking, I hope she doesn't actually mean that she wants me to get her into my reunion. The truth is, I'm looking forward to seeing all my friends from my student days, but if Nicola comes, I'll end up keeping her company all night.

'It's fine. I'll just drink by myself. Don't worry about me,' she says, although only slightly sarcastically.

'Why don't you get yourself a date lined up?' I suggest. 'It's been a while since your last one.'

That's an understatement. It's been months since Nicola dated a guy, and I'm not really sure why she seems to have stopped. I would love it if she got herself a boyfriend, and I know Tom would too. At least that way, we could do double dates as opposed to Nicola and I going out while Tom sits home alone.

'If only it were that easy. We don't all have men throwing themselves at us like you do.'

'I do not have men throwing themselves at me.'

'Are you kidding? Even when you were single, you always had some guy on the go.'

She's not wrong there. But so what? I enjoyed myself before I got engaged. She could do the same. It's not as if I'm any prettier than she is.

'There's plenty of guys who would love to go on a date with you,' I remind my friend as I grab my towel and a bottle of shampoo and prepare to hit the showers. 'And if not, there's always Peter the Pervert.'

'Oi!' Nicola cries as I run into the showers before she can hit me with her towel, laughing as I go.

## 10

## THE BOYFRIEND

This university campus is foreign to me yet a little familiar at the same time. I have never been a student here, I never attended lectures here, and I certainly never enjoyed an evening in the bar here. Yet I recognise some of the buildings from the photos I saw online from when I looked this place up many years ago.

I had to do my research to find out where Adele was studying, didn't I?

Now she is back here again, visiting this campus for a reunion with all her old uni friends, and I can see her from where I am standing, watching her laughing and joking with all these graduates. She can't see me of course, I'm too far away from her for that, and there's plenty of people standing in between us, so there is no chance of me being caught. That's good because I should not be here. I don't belong here. I am not an ex-student.

I am only here because Adele is.

*I wonder who the tall guy is whom she is talking to now, keeping my eyes on the distance between the pair of them and wondering if it is going to get any smaller. They are certainly enjoying their interaction if their wide smiles are anything to go by. But then Adele accepts a drink from a female friend and walks away, leaving the tall man to watch her go, no doubt disappointed that she is exiting his life.*

*I know how he feels.*

*Adele is on the move, so I should be too. Maintaining a safe distance, I track her through the crowded room, keeping my head low and hoping that nobody stops me and asks me who I am. It was easy to sneak into this reunion because nobody asked for a ticket or any form of identification. I simply arrived at the venue early, told the guy on the desk that it was weird to be back here after all these years, and he smiled at me and told me where I could get a drink. All I had to do then was find a quiet corner and wait for the room to fill up, keeping my eyes peeled for the arrival of the woman who I knew would be here tonight.*

*I have not looked away from Adele ever since she got here, not even when a random woman came up to me and asked me if I was some guy called Chris who used to be on her biology course with her. I simply shook my head and told her that she had me mixed up with somebody else, and she left, shrugging her shoulders and no doubt disappointed that she still hadn't found her old classmate. But her level of disappointment could never match mine at losing what I once had.*

*I only have to look at Adele to feel that.*

*She seems to be having a good time so far, enjoying her evening catching up with old friends. But I'm enjoying my evening too. It's impossible not to when I am in the same place as her. I could watch her for hours. I have done and I will continue to do so.*

*I will keep watching her.*

*And as always, she will have no idea that I am here.*

## 11

It feels like yesterday when I was walking around this place and not the fifteen years that it actually is. The university campus has changed a lot since I was last here, but there are still some parts of it that I recognise. Like the giant sculpture that stands in the centre of the campus square: every student who studies here has an obligatory photo taken beside it at some point. Or the stone steps at the front of the library, where many a sunny weekday afternoon is spent with friends, eating, drinking, and generally lazing around like only a student can. But most of the buildings have been revamped and refreshed since I was last here, which has taken the shine off my reminiscing as I stroll around the campus and think back over my three happy years as a student.

The reunion that commenced in the student union bar at seven started out as a quiet and slightly awkward affair, as it took old friends a while to become reacquainted. But just like it had done on our very first day here when we were eighteen, alcohol made things much easier, and it wasn't long until everybody was laughing and joking like we'd never been apart. I've had a great time catching up with my best friends from my uni days, hearing what everyone has been up to since we all grew up and became proper adults, and I definitely don't regret coming here tonight. But there is a tinge of sadness about it, which was noted by one of the guys who made a short but touching speech about Calum, the old friend we sadly lost only a week before this night.

Being back here has obviously stirred up all sorts of memories for me, and it's been impossible not to think about Calum, especially now as I walk past so many of the areas in which we used to hang out together when we were dating. The sports fields where we would lie on sunny days, kissing and wondering if life could get any easier than it was right then. Or the various lecture halls we would walk to together before going our separate ways for the day, counting down the hours until we were back by each other's side. I have so many memories wrapped up in this place, and likewise, so many memories of good times attached to Calum. It really is a shame he isn't here tonight.

But it wasn't as if I spent all my time as a student being loved up. In between ending things with Shaun and starting a relationship with Calum, I made the most of being young, free, and single. One-night stands were not unusual, although my memory when it comes to most of those is certainly not as sharp as it is in remembering other things. I'm slightly ashamed to say that if I was pressed for a number on how many men I have been intimate with in my life, I would struggle to give an accurate answer. I blame that on all the cheap drinks that the bars and nightclubs in this city liked to offer to students. It's not easy to remember a guy's name if you only spent one night with him and all that time occurred under the influence of such memory-mashing liquids as tequila, vodka, or the dreaded gin. I do wish I could recall their names and faces better, but there is a black hole of sorts in my memory when it comes to that time period.

Never mind.

If I couldn't enjoy myself at uni, then when could I?

'I'm glad there are no students here tonight. I already feel ancient enough as it is without seeing their supple skin to make me feel even worse.'

I laugh at the comment from Alicia, one of my best friends from my course and a woman whom I have kept in semi-regular contact with since graduation. Back in those days, she was even wilder than I was, but amazingly, she is now a lawyer who stands up in front of judges on a daily basis and defends criminals. Based on what I know about her, I find it hilarious that anybody would put their trust in her, never mind somebody hoping to avoid prison. In fact, there were several points in our youth when I was convinced that prison would be the best place for her.

'I know what you mean,' I reply, taking a sip of the cheap drink that I purchased in the student union before we went on this little walk around the campus. 'The three-day hangover after today is enough to remind me of my age. I definitely don't need an eighteen-year-old to do it for me.'

We walk on, laughing and joking about old times until we come to a place that we both recognise well. It's the huge hall that hosted the graduation ball, and it's the place where Calum and I famously did a dance routine in front of everybody in attendance. Calum was quite the mover and had competed in amateur dance competitions in his teens and he never missed an opportunity to get me to dance with him.

'Oh, my, that dance was epic,' Alicia says just after I have recalled it. 'I wish I still had the video of it.'

'I would have paid you to burn it if you did,' I reply, shuddering at how cringeworthy it must have been.

We laugh as we take a seat on a bench opposite the hall before Alicia speaks again.

'You know, back then, I was convinced that you two were going to get married and have lots of kids together,' she says.

'I don't know about that,' I say, shaking my head. 'But we had fun together. He was a great guy.'

'Yeah, he was. I hope his family sue the car company for his death.'

I nod my head, hoping for the same thing too, not that it would do much good in bringing Calum back. But it sounds like his family might have a case if they were to pursue one. The media reports surrounding Calum's death have referred to a failure with the brakes, resulting in him losing control of his car and skidding off the road, unable to stop. It's terribly bad luck, and while it was fortunate that no other car was involved, that's not much consolation to those whom Calum has left behind.

'I always wonder about fate,' Alicia says after a sombre moment. 'Like was he meant to die that night in that way? Was there nothing he could have done to avoid it? He was so happy that night dancing in there with you. Could things have been any different?'

I nod because I have wondered the same thing too, and not just since two of my exes have died. Do I have control over what happens to me in the future, or is my fate already sealed, one way or another, and I just don't know it yet?

'Who knows?' I say, finishing my drink and getting up off the wall because I'm ready to go in search of another. 'But it's definitely the worst thing about getting older, isn't it? Being more aware of death and all that stuff?'

'Yeah,' Alicia agrees. 'I can't argue with you there.'

We walk away from the hall back in the direction of the bar, and while I have no doubt that the rest of the night will be filled with more light-hearted thoughts and conversations than this, there is no denying that what Alicia and I have just said is true. Forget bad hang-overs, worrying wrinkles, and a need to save money instead of blowing it – the worst part of ageing is the realisation that life isn't as endless as it initially seemed to be. There's nothing quite like a couple of shocking deaths to remind someone of their mortality, and as I re-enter the bar and see all the laughing faces around me, I can't help but think of Shaun and Calum and about how they have been robbed of making any more memories.

Life is short, there is no question about it. The only question I have is when will my time be up? I'd like to think I have plenty of years left in me yet, but I guess so does everybody else. In reality, none of us know.

With that in mind, I'm just going to enjoy myself as much as I can, for as long as I can.

Starting tonight.

## 12

I was wrong. My hangover after the reunion didn't last for three days.

It has lasted for four.

I feel like I haven't been able to get a good night's sleep since that heavy night on the weekend, and if there was any doubt before then, it has been removed now. I really am getting old. But there's no time for feeling sorry for myself today – I have important work to do with Tom. We're off to see another wedding venue, and I'm just hoping that this visit goes well because we are quickly running out of potential places to host our wedding. All the venues that were at the top of our list a couple of weeks ago have since been either chalked off willingly or begrudgingly since we started to get a better idea of dates, prices, and what they could or could not offer us.

Slater's had no availability until next autumn, which is frustrating because we have our hearts set on a summer wedding. Church Lane have put their fees up suddenly, pricing us out unless either of us is willing to sell an organ on the black market, which we aren't. And even Prior House, an old stately home that we thought might be a viable option, has been crossed off the list since there was an article in the local newspaper about their finances being mismanaged, meaning there is no guarantee they might be able to host a wedding by the time it comes around.

With not much else to choose from in the area, we were almost at the point of looking further afield when Tom suggested the venue that we have just arrived at now.

Heron's Barn.

There's no doubt it is a beautiful property and certainly one suited to hosting a picture-perfect wedding, but as I mentioned to Nicola back when I started looking, I ruled this place out because the wedding planner here is Rachel, my ex-best friend. But desperate times call for desperate measures if we want to find somewhere local before all the best dates are gone, so here we are, sitting patiently in the reception area and waiting for Rachel to appear.

'It's going to be fine,' Tom whispers to me after noticing how much I have been fidgeting with my handbag for the last five minutes.

He knows why I am nervous about this meeting, although he doesn't seem to think it is as big a deal as I do. 'So what if you used to know Rachel?' he had said before I reluctantly made this appointment. 'I'm sure she's a professional and will just be happy to help you, regardless of any history between the pair of you, and it's not as if you actually fell out, is it? You just drifted apart.'

I had wanted to tell my fiancé that it wasn't always as simple as that, particularly when it came to the break-up of female friendships, but I decided not to waste my time. Tom doesn't understand how things like this can be awkward because he has a couple of old friends who talk about nothing more than football and pub crawls, and that's about the extent of his 'complicated social life'. But mine has been more eventful, and today is just another example of that.

I hear the sound of the high heels on the marble floor coming towards me before I see her, but I already know by the pace of the walk that it will be her. Rachel was always a fast walker, and I spent a lot of time trying to catch up with her back when we were friends and hanging out all the time. Sure enough, I look to my left and see her, looking very professional in a white blouse and black knee-length skirt. She is also clutching a clipboard, which I expect contains all sorts of notes about this venue and how it can cater to a potential wedding like ours.

As she gets nearer, I wonder if she is going to treat me like the old friend I used to be or if she will be all business, but I don't have to wait long to get my answer.

'Adele! Great to see you! And this must be your fiancé! How nice to meet you!'

Rachel has a huge smile plastered across her face that could be real or fake, but there's not much time to try to figure it out before she gives us both a big hug and shows us into a private meeting room.

As we take our seats, Tom gives me a look as if to say I had nothing to worry about, but I'm still feeling unsure about this whole thing as Rachel takes out a pen and prepares to plan our wedding.

Fortunately, the overly friendly greeting we got that had me feeling a little bad about not wanting to try here makes way for a calmer and more professional demeanour, and the next sixty minutes is spent discussing facts and figures. Surprisingly, this venue not only has the ideal date we would like but is very reasonably priced and can even cater to my slightly eccentric demand that all the hospitality staff wear pink to fit in with the colour scheme. Not only that, but Rachel is showing no signs of awkwardness towards me, just like at Shaun's funeral, although I do wish she hadn't brought it up just after we had sat down. Referring to one of my exes in front of the man I am preparing to marry wasn't the smartest move on her part, but she quickly recovered and moved on.

Now the meeting is coming to an end, and everything seems like it is going well. We haven't committed to anything yet because we need time to discuss it, but the few telling glances I shared with my fiancé throughout Rachel's 'pitch' has obviously offered up a clue to how we are feeling, so Rachel seems confident enough to go ahead and say what's on her mind.

'I always knew I'd get an invite to your wedding, one way or another.'

'I'm sorry?' I say, a little confused.

'I'll be at your wedding if you choose to have it here. As the wedding planner, of course.'

'Oh, right,' I reply, laughing a little awkwardly.

I'm surprised she has felt the need to say that, and while it hasn't ruined all the good work that she has done in selling us on this venue, it has put a little dampener on the day in my mind. The thought of having my ex-best friend watching me celebrating with my current best friend in Nicola would be very weird. I'm sure Rachel would think that it could have been her fulfilling the duties of my maid of honour if things had worked out differently.

'I'm not sure if Adele told you, but we used to be best friends,' Rachel says, smiling at Tom.

'She did mention it, actually,' he replies with an excellent poker face.

'Yeah, proper besties back in the day, weren't we?'

I laugh a little nervously and nod. 'Yeah, back in primary school,' I say, somehow feeling like it is important to reference precisely how long ago it was, though I'm not sure why.

'I thought seeing you at the funeral was weird,' Rachel goes on, seemingly growing in confidence. 'But seeing you again now so soon, it's almost as if we were meant to come back into each other's lives, don't you think?'

I smile, not wanting to be rude but also not sure what she is getting at. What started off as a slightly awkward meeting is quickly descending into an extremely uncomfortable one.

Does she want to be my friend again? Is that it?

'It's been lovely to see you again,' I say, nodding my head as if I need to convince her.

'Hasn't it? We should go for a drink sometime. No pressure. Even if you decide not to have your wedding here. What do you think?'

I realise that to say no to such a suggestion would just seem downright rude, so I smile and say that would be lovely. Then we finally wrap up the meeting and say our goodbyes, promising Rachel that we will be in touch about the wedding, although it's obvious she is more bothered about the drink we might have instead.

'I don't know what you were worried about. She's lovely,' Tom says to me as we get into our car, and he slots the key into the ignition.

I'm just about to answer him when I see two messages on my mobile phone. I put it on silent while we were in the meeting, so I haven't checked it for a while, and now that I have, I wish I hadn't.

The first one is from a girl I used to know from my

backpacking days, and while it would usually be lovely to hear from her, today she comes bearing bad news.

There's been another death, and yes, it's another one of my exes.

It's a guy called Ryan, and apparently he died in a house fire.

But it's the second message that is even more shocking. It has come from a number I don't recognise, but what it says brings back all the feelings of doubt and worry after the death of my first two boyfriends.

*Three down. Three to go.*

## 13

Ryan Harris came into my life at a time when I thought I already had everything. I was twenty-five, healthy, happy, and completely unencumbered by all the things that seemed to be weighing down almost everybody I had left behind in England. While they were all sitting in traffic on their way to do a job they hated or saving up money for a house that would tie them down both financially and geographically, I was moving from one place to another, bouncing across the map as if the planet were my own personal playground.

Maybe it was. It certainly felt that way when I was scuba diving in the Solomon Islands and watching the sunset in Singapore. And when I was bodyboarding in Bali and making memories in Melbourne. Altogether, I was overseas and perfecting my beach-bum/backpacker persona for two years, taking in dozens of new countries and cultures, funded by my casual work in bars and hostels, as I did anything I could to avoid the two-word phrases that I hated the most – 'settling down' and 'growing up'.

I only had two words to say back to that at the time. 'No, thanks.'

But if there was one thing that could remind me that there was more to life than just plane-hopping and sightseeing, it was that little thing called love.

I was standing behind a bar in Auckland, New Zealand, when I first laid eyes on him. He walked into the busy venue with an easy smile and a confident posture, and by the time he made his way over to me to order a drink, I'd decided that I wanted to get to know him more. But that wasn't an easy thing to do then because I still had four hours left of my shift. Unlike the rest of the young women in that place, all of whom were drinking merrily and dancing salaciously, I had to stand behind the bar, serve drinks, and smile.

But then something wonderful happened. This guy whom I liked and had watched walk in told me that he liked my Northern English accent, which made me smile. Then he told me he liked my smile too, and by then, I was putty in his hands. But I still hadn't expected anything to happen. All I could do was serve him and wait for him to hit the dance floor with all my love rivals in there that night. But that didn't happen, at least not him leaving me to dance with other girls. I did serve him, several times in fact, but he stayed by the bar and kept me company for the rest of my shift, amusing himself with his requests for me to say certain words in my accent so he could hear what they sounded like. In return, I did the same thing to him, asking him to demonstrate the full range of his Northern Irish accent, until before we knew it, my shift was over, the bar was almost empty, and he was asking me what I was doing afterwards.

I told him that I was willing to do whatever he was doing too, which was how we ended up down by the harbour until sunrise, drinking, sharing our travelling stories and, eventually, kissing as the sky turned from black to blue.

I saw Ryan almost every day for the next month, as I continued to save up for the next part of my travels while he did the same until the time came for me to pack my backpack again. I'd arranged to meet friends in America, where my around-the-world adventures would continue. But I didn't want to go. I wanted to stay with Ryan, even though I knew he was going to be leaving soon for his own adventures in Asia. That was the problem. We were two kindred spirits who had fallen in love because we shared a passion for travel, yet now it was that very thing that was going to tear us apart.

It was an emotional goodbye when it came, and there were kisses and tears at Auckland International before we walked away from each other. We felt sad but blessed as we parted, whilst also carrying a hope that our paths would cross again one day somewhere on this wonderful planet that we were both fully determined to explore.

And sure enough, they did.

It was in New York when we saw each other again, messages over social media ensuring that we were ready when the time came for both of us to be in the same place at the same time. Our next rendezvous was in Rio, a couple of days after the Carnival. And there were several more meetups in equally glamorous places around the globe over the next eighteen months, as we both kept travelling and 'bumping into each other'. Eventually, we decided to dispense with the silly notion of saying goodbye only to say hello again months later, deciding to travel together instead. We toured Europe in a camper van and spent six weeks trekking through parts of Africa, which I probably wouldn't recommend in hindsight because of how dangerous it was. But we didn't care at the time – we were young, adventurous, and, most of all, in love with each other.

But then it ended, only this time I wasn't the one to do the dumping.

It was on a steaming hot night in South Africa, sitting under a starry sky, when I said the words that I never thought I would say. I told Ryan that I was thinking about going home and settling down. After years on the road, living out of a backpack and never having more than a thousand pounds to my name at any one time, I was finally starting to grow weary of all the uncertainty. I'd seen it all, and now I wanted some stability. The only thing I was uncertain about was if Ryan wanted the same thing.

Unfortunately, he did not, and he told me as much, politely but firmly. He said that he never saw himself returning to the UK, and while he knew he would settle down somewhere one day, he had no idea when and where.

At that moment, I knew exactly how Shaun and Calum must have felt when I ended things with them.

Sad. Confused. And terribly lonely.

I tried to change his mind, just like my previous exes had tried with me during our break-ups. But just like I had in my past, Ryan stuck solidly to his decision, and in the end, all we could do was say goodbye.

Returning home after so many years away was tough, but that was nothing compared to how I felt when I would go online and see photos that Ryan had shared from whichever exotic location he was in that day. I had thought about not only deleting him from my list of friends so that I wouldn't have to see them but also deleting all the photos the two of us had shared during our travels together. My social media pages were full of them. But I decided not to in the end, and in hindsight, I was glad of that because those were special years in my life, and he was a big part of it. Therefore, he deserved to stay a part of it.

Ryan was true to his word after our break-up, continuing to travel, and I followed his adventures from afar for years, until one day I saw that he was getting married to a pretty Englishwoman he had met in the Maldives. But he was wrong about one thing. He did return to the UK, setting up home in Portsmouth, where it isn't far to make the crossing to Calais, where many Brits go to start their adventures in Europe, as I once had done many years ago.

I hadn't heard any more about him until today when I found out that he had died in a house fire on the south coast, his body discovered amongst the burnt-out remains of the property he shared with his wife. Fortunately, she wasn't home with him at the time the fire started, otherwise she would have perished too, but poor Ryan was gone, and that makes it a hat-trick of ex-boyfriends I have lost recently.

If I thought it was weird before, now I'm certain something is very wrong.

But I don't just need to trust my intuition anymore.

I have that text message to confirm it.

*Three down. Three to go.*

To anybody else, that message might have meant nothing. But to me, coming on the day that the news of Ryan's death broke, I knew exactly what it meant.

Three down? Shaun. Calum. Ryan.

My first three boyfriends are dead, and I'm guessing

whoever sent me this message saw to that. But what about three to go?

At first, I thought maybe I was reading it wrong because I only have two more exes. Ash and Jesse. But then I figured it out.

My sixth boyfriend is my current one.

*Tom will be the last.*

I haven't said anything to him. I haven't even said a word to anybody. But I need to do something soon because now I know the truth.

These deaths aren't random. They are planned.

And they obviously aren't over yet.

## 14

After a couple of hours of thinking about it, I've decided what I'm going to do. I'm going to go to the police, show them the text message and get them to look further into the deaths of my three exes as well as provide protection to Ash, Jesse, and, most importantly, Tom. This message proves that there is somebody out there picking off my old boyfriends one by one, so I need to act now before anybody else gets hurt. I also need to do it for those whom I am too late to save.

Shaun, Calum, and Ryan deserve justice, and that is what I will get them.

But first, I need to tell Tom where I am about to go.

I walk into the bedroom and find my fiancé sitting on the carpet with a large box of tools beside him and several pieces of wood, which don't look like much at the moment but will make a very pretty bedside table when they are all fitted together. Bless him, as if he doesn't work hard enough, he's now doing DIY in his spare time.

Normally, I'd be more than happy to leave him to it,

but now that I have figured out what I need to do regarding the mysterious text message, I cannot wait a second longer. I'm going to the police station. The only thing I need to know is if Tom is willing to come with me.

'I need to show you something,' I say as I take a seat on the edge of the bed and hold out my phone towards Tom, but he ignores it and keeps working.

'Just let me finish this, and I'll be right with you,' he says, slotting another screw into a hole in the wood.

'No, I need to tell you. It can't wait.'

'Really?'

'Tom, please!'

The desperate edge to my voice does enough to get him to lower his screwdriver and finally look at me.

'What is it?' he asks as he takes my phone from me and looks at the screen.

'It's a text message I got earlier.'

'Three down, three to go. What does that mean?'

'I think it's talking about my boyfriends?'

'What?'

I take a deep breath and prepare to explain my crazy theory to him. I know it's going to be difficult, but I see this as a practise run before I have to do the same thing with the police. It will be a good test too, because if I can't convince Tom that something is wrong, then I might have a hard time convincing a copper too.

'You know I told you about Shaun?'

'The guy who hanged himself?'

I pause and not just because of the fairly blunt question my fiancé has just asked. Now I'm not sure it was suicide.

'Yeah. Well, you know how he was my first boyfriend?'

Tom reluctantly nods.

'Well, not only has he died recently, but my second and third boyfriends have died too.'

'What?'

Maybe I should have told him about Ryan's death on the way back from the wedding venue. I definitely should have told him about Calum's death by now because that was a week ago. But here goes. Better late than never.

'The guy I dated at university, Calum, he died in a car accident last week. And today, I found out that Ryan, my third boyfriend, whom I met while I was travelling, died in a house fire in Portsmouth.'

Tom frowns, but it's a different look to the one he wears when he is doing DIY. It's a frown that suggests he is having trouble keeping up with me, but I carry on anyway.

'I know it sounds like all these deaths are accidents or whatever. But three of my exes all within a couple of weeks of each other? That can't be a coincidence, can it? And then there's that text message. Three down, three to go. It has to be referring to those deaths, right?'

I end my wittering with a question for Tom – even though I am sure that there is a problem, I still feel like I need him to tell me that I am right. But he doesn't answer me. Instead, he just returns my phone to me and goes back to making the bedside table.

'I didn't realise you had so many boyfriends,' he says eventually, and it's clear he wants it to sound casual because he doesn't stop working as he does.

'What are you talking about? I told you about all my boyfriends.'

'Nope, I didn't know about one at uni. And I certainly didn't know you had six.'

It takes me a second to realise that he is referring to the message again, but he doesn't understand.

'Tom, I had five boyfriends, and I have told you about them all. But this message says six, so I think it means the last one is you.'

That does enough to get him to stop screwing for one moment before he shakes his head and carries on again.

'So what are you saying? All your boyfriends are going to die?'

When he puts it like that, it does sound crazy. Yet that's exactly what I'm getting at.

'I think so,' I reply, although I've lost a little conviction since I first walked in here, and Tom must pick up on that because he laughs.

'Have you been drinking with Nicola again?' he asks sarcastically, but I'm hurt he would even make any kind of joke when he can surely see how worried I am.

'Tom, I'm being serious. Three of my exes are already dead.'

'And what did you say were the cause of deaths? Suicide, car crash, and house fire? It doesn't sound like murder to me.'

'Maybe it was made to look that way! The message has to mean something.'

'It could mean anything. It might even have been meant for somebody else, and they sent it to you by mistake.'

'No, it wasn't.'

'How do you know?'

'Because I texted them back asking if it was, and they didn't reply.'

'You texted them back?'

'Yes! And I called them. But they didn't pick up.'

'Probably because it was a wrong number, and they didn't want to waste their time.'

I shake my head, dismayed that Tom doesn't believe

me but refusing to back down and entertain the idea that all these deaths were just unfortunate incidents with no connection. I know there is a connection between them all. *Me.*

'I'm going to go to the police. I just wanted to speak to you about it first,' I say, getting up off the bed and heading for the doorway.

'You're doing what?' Tom asks, dropping his screwdriver and allowing a piece of wood to clatter down onto the piece beneath it.

'I have to do something. People are in danger.'

'Your exes, you mean?'

'Well, yes, but you as well.'

Tom shakes his head. 'All of this from a text message? You're being ridiculous.'

'What else am I supposed to do? Wait for the next one to die?'

'I don't know, but I'm beginning to think you're more concerned about them than you are about me.'

'What the hell is that supposed to mean?'

'What I mean is all I have heard about lately is guys you used to go out with. Like Shaun. You went to his funeral without telling me. How do you think that made me feel?'

'I said sorry!'

'And now here you are telling me about some other guys that you used to date, including some guy at university who I definitely didn't even know existed. Did you go to his funeral as well? Was the reunion just a cover story so you could go and say goodbye to him too?'

I'm incredulous. Is he really accusing me of caring about my exes more than him?

'Well?' he says, looking at me from his position on the carpet, surrounded by tools and pieces of wood that

I almost wish I could pick up and throw at him. But instead, I take the sensible option, which is walking out of the bedroom.

I don't even bother saying goodbye to him.

I just leave the house, get in the car and set off in the direction of the police station.

## 15

I thought my plan was a good one until I arrived at the station.

As I stood at the front desk and looked through the glass at the police officer behind it, I wasn't sure whom to ask for. A detective who specialised in cracking murder cases? Or just any police officer who might be able to give me some advice about how to keep my fiancé alive?

Maybe it was the blow to my confidence that my argument with Tom had dealt me, but the longer I stood there, hesitating and tripping over my words, the more I realised I was out of my depth.

In the end, I think the officer on the front desk took pity on me because she told me to take a seat and that somebody would come and speak to me soon. Bless her, she probably had no idea what it was I was talking about in amongst my confused mumblings about ex-boyfriends, text messages, and needing to warn other people, and the longer I wait here now, the less certain I am too.

I really wish Tom were here with me. Just having

him beside me would be all the support I needed to get through whatever is going to happen next, even if he was only humouring me and didn't believe any of this himself. But sadly, he is not here; instead he's still at home, where I left him after we both raised our voices at each other in a disagreement about what I feel is something deadly serious. But maybe it doesn't matter that Tom didn't believe me that there was something to worry about. The important thing is that the police do because they're the only ones who can actually do something about it. Of course, it matters on some level that Tom hasn't taken my side, but that's more a matter for our relationship.

Right now, in this police station, this is a matter of life and death.

The officer who comes to speak to me ten minutes later is a polite but very young man, at least ten years my junior and someone who looks more like the guys I used to party with in my travelling days than a person tasked with upholding the law around here. But I know I shouldn't hold his age against him as I follow him into a small room and take a seat opposite him at a table. The uniform he is wearing is enough to tell me that he has to take my claims seriously, which is all that matters, and as we take our seats, I smile at PC Brown and prepare to get started.

I decide to adopt a slightly different tactic this time as opposed to the way I broached this conversation with Tom earlier. Instead of starting with the text message, I lead with Shaun's 'suicide', an incident I presume the police officer is already aware of, as it happened not far from here. Then I quickly run over Calum's and Ryan's deaths, highlighting the fact that each person who died was once close to me and that there is a definite sequence that seems to be being adhered to. Then I mention the fact that I have two more ex-boyfriends, still alive but potentially in danger, before concluding with my biggest concern, which is that my current partner and fiancé may also be at risk too. Lastly, and before the police officer has the chance to do what Tom did and try to disparage what I have just said, I show him the message, which now has some definite context given to it after all I have told him.

The thirty seconds or so that I have to wait in silence while the police officer reads and rereads the text message are some of the longest seconds of my life.

'Have you received any other communication from this number?' PC Brown asks me.

'No, just the text message,' I confirm, feeling a wave of optimism. It seems like I'm at least being taken seriously here. But that's quickly tempered by the next words out of the young man's mouth.

'Without anything else to put this message with, it doesn't prove what it actually relates to.'

I stare at the officer, praying that there has to be something I can say to get him to take me seriously.

'I just told you what it relates to. My relationships. I've had six serious ones in my life, including my current one. Three down, three to go. What else could it mean?'

'To be honest, it could mean anything.'

'What?'

'This message could mean anything. It could be talking about something at work, or be some kind of joke, or it could even have been meant for somebody else and was just sent to the wrong number by mistake.'

'No! It was obviously meant for me, and it obviously refers to my three ex-boyfriends who have died in the last fortnight!'

I'm aware I'm getting louder and realise it's probably not a wise thing to do to shout at a police officer, but I can't help it. I know I'm right, but it's not much good if nobody else knows it too.

Fortunately, the man I am having this conversation with now is a lot calmer than my fiancé, and he holds his tongue before responding, giving me enough time to simmer down and stop this descending into an argument.

'Look, I can see you're very worked up about this, and I understand. Losing three people from your past so close together must be very difficult for you, and I'm sorry about that.'

I take a deep breath and thank PC Brown for his kind words before I let him go on.

'But right now, if all you are basing your claims on is this text message, then it's going to be very difficult to prove anything more sinister is going on.'

'Can't you look into the deaths? It is possible for somebody to fake a suicide, right? Somebody might have hanged Shaun from that tree. And Calum's car crash. What if somebody tampered with the brakes?'

'And the house fire that killed Ryan? You think somebody started that too?'

'Yes!'

PC Brown takes a long moment to consider his next words, giving me enough time to suppress my emotions again after they threatened to spill out.

'Okay, I'll see if I can get someone to take another look at Shaun's death. But Calum's might be trickier, as it was in a different part of the country. The same goes for Ryan.'

'Just look into them, please. I know something is wrong.'

PC Brown nods his head, although it's clear from the look on his face that he has more sympathy for me than any of the victims I have just talked about. He feels sorry for me, like I'm some madwoman who has clearly lost her grip on reality after one silly text message.

'Is there anything else?' he asks me, sliding my mobile phone back across the table.

'Yes,' I say, picking it up and dropping it back into my handbag. 'If I'm right, then you need to get somebody to look after my other boyfriends. Ash Sweeney would be next. I'm not sure on his address, but you can message him on social media. He's on all the usual platforms. And then there's Jesse Addams. You should actually have him in your system because he was arrested once for being violent towards me and—'

'One of your exes was violent?'

'Yeah, it was a few years ago.'

'Do you think he might be behind this?'

'Who, Jesse? No, the text message obviously included him in the six. And then there's my fiancé, Tom. I need you to have somebody look out for him in case I am right and he's in danger too.'

'Whoa, slow down. You're going very fast. First of all, like I said, I'll see if I can get somebody to take another look into Shaun's death. If we do find anything suspicious after looking again, then we'll be in touch.'

'No, we might not have time! You need to protect these men now!'

'From whom?'

PC Brown's question is a simple one, but he must know that I have no answer.

'I don't know,' I admit, feeling like I've just lost all momentum in trying to convince him to see things my way again.

'Exactly,' he says, although he at least looks at me like he cares, unlike Tom, who looked at me like I was the one in the wrong.

I lower my eyes to the table between us and wish I had something else to offer the police in their investigation, if we can even call it that at this stage. But I don't. I have nothing.

'Let's just say you are right,' PC Brown says. 'And I'm not saying you are, and I'm definitely not saying you or your fiancé have anything to worry about. But if there is somebody out there picking off your ex-boyfriends, then it has to be somebody who knows about them all, right?'

I look up from the table at the calming blue eyes of PC Brown and realise he has a point.

'So who knows about all your boyfriends? Who have you told?'

I think about the answer to that question, but the immediate answers it throws up are of little help.

'I don't know. My family, I guess. And my best friends.'

'And your current partner?'

PC Brown's suggestion is not a welcome one, but it is valid. I have told Tom all about my exes, even if he pretended not to know about Calum from my uni days. But he wouldn't have anything to do with this. Nor would my friends or my family.

'Well, yeah, he knows about them. But he wouldn't be doing this,' I say, shaking my head.

'Look, I'm sure this is just a series of unfortunate events that will hopefully end now without any more tragic loss of life,' PC Brown says. 'But while we look into what we can, you could also help by figuring out who might be behind that message. If this is true, then it has to be somebody you know, right? How else would they know about all your boyfriends?'

## 16

PC Brown's last words to me are still rattling around in my head as I wait for Nicola to join me in this quiet bar. She's late again, although I suppose this time she does have a genuine excuse. I only messaged her about meeting up an hour ago, so it is rather last minute. But thankfully, she agreed, which I'm glad about because after the day I have had, I needed a drink.

And right now, I need another one.

I get up from my seat and head to the bar again, ordering another glass of white wine and giving the bored-looking guy opposite me something to do. It's still quite early, so this venue is almost empty, not that I'm going to let that put me off getting started.

'Actually, scrap that. How much is it for a bottle?' I ask the barman, and I give him a nod of the head to proceed after he gives me the price. To be honest, I barely even acknowledge his answer – I would have agreed to it whatever it was.

As I receive the bottle and carry it back to my table in the corner, I think about calling Tom and telling him where I am in case he is worrying, before I remember how he spoke to me the last time we were together. With that in mind, I keep my phone in my handbag and proceed to pour myself another glass of wine. He can worry all he wants. I'm certainly doing enough of that for myself after my visit to the police station.

PC Brown was kind enough to promise me that he would have somebody take another look into Shaun's death to make sure that it was suicide and nothing more sinister, although I'm not holding out much hope with regard to that. I'm sure if somebody did kill him, then they would have gone to great lengths to make it look right, and the police obviously didn't notice anything unusual at the time. Considering it's already been a fortnight since the body was found and no suspicions appear to have been raised, other than from me, any killer must have done a good job of it. But perhaps there may be clues or mistakes to be found in Calum's and Ryan's deaths, and at least now somebody knows to go looking for them. But it was PC Brown's words about a potential suspect that had the greatest impact on me. He says if I am right, and it is a big if, then the potential suspect has to be someone close to me; otherwise how would they know whom to target?

Hearing something like that from a police officer would be enough to send anybody into a spiral of self-doubt and paranoia, and I'm no different, which explains why I'm now sitting in a pub drinking by myself. But I'm not going to cut myself off from every-body, despite PC Brown's suggestion that any potential murderer I have might be very close to home. While I have no idea who could be behind these deaths, I am sure of a few things. There is no way anyone in my family is involved. Likewise, Tom would not be behind this – while he might disagree with me on things from time to time, he's a good person, and he loves me. So too does my best friend, Nicola, which is why I am meeting her now. I need somebody to debrief with after my visit to the station, and she is my best bet. If I speak to my parents about this, then they will only worry. If I speak to Tom, then we're risking another argument. That's why Nicola is the better option. She will just listen and give a balanced opinion at the end of it, unlike the others.

I'm just about to pour my second glass from the bottle when Nicola walks in, her hair looking wet from the drizzle that is falling outside.

'Is everything okay? Has something happened with the wedding?' she asks me before she has even sat down.

I'm surprised she has jumped to the conclusion that something must have gone wrong with my upcoming nuptials to Tom until I remember that I had told her about my appointment at Heron's Barn today. She has clearly put two and two together and come up with five, presuming that something bad happened at the meeting, and now my wedding might not be happening. Bless her, she's a good friend, but she doesn't always get it right.

'I'm okay. And so is the wedding,' I tell her, giving her a quick hug before we sit down, and I pour her a glass from my open bottle.

'So what is it?' she asks before taking a thirsty sip.

'I've just been to the police station,' I tell her before quickly but precisely running through everything I said to PC Brown in that room. When I'm finished, Nicola's eyes are almost as wide as the rim of her wine glass.

'You think somebody is killing all your exes?' she asks me as she reads the mysterious text message I received earlier.

'Yeah, I do,' I reply, carefully studying my friend's face for her reaction. It's important that she believes me because Tom obviously doesn't, and I fear that PC Brown was just being polite and humouring me. But Nicola has to be on my side. Doesn't she?

'How much wine have you had?' she asks me, handing back my phone and eyeing me sceptically.

I can tell she is joking, but I'm not in the mood to laugh, and she quickly realises that.

'Nic, I'm serious. Something is wrong here. You believe me, don't you?'

'Of course I do,' she says, and it's a relief when she reaches out her hand towards mine and gives it a squeeze. 'It's just a lot to wrap my head around.'

'I understand.'

'You really think Shaun was murdered?'

'Possibly. It could have been made to look like he killed himself.'

Nicola nods. 'And the other two?'

'Same. Somebody could have killed them and just made it look like an accident.'

Nicola ruminates on my statement for a moment before picking up her wine glass and shrugging her shoulders.

'I think we're going to need another bottle,' she says, and I laugh, feeling at least a little of the tension from the day leaving my body, although all the alcohol I have already consumed is playing its part, I'm sure. But this is just what I needed. Somebody who not only believes me but is fully on my side. Nicola is a good friend, but I need her to be more than that now.

I need her to help me figure out what to do next.

## 17

I'm not sure how conducive a couple of bottles of wine are to making a solid plan, but Nicola and I are doing our best to find out. The drinks are flowing easily, which is more than can be said for our ideas, which have been limited, to say the least.

So far, we have debated the identity of any potential killer and come up with nothing. No spurned exes. No jilted lovers. Not even guys who might have held a grudge against me after I failed to message them back after a date because I always messaged back, even if it was just to be polite. I've gone through every single male I can ever remember being intimate with in my life, and none of them strikes me as being the kind of man who could be jealous or vengeful enough to put into motion something like this. While there are a few nights from my past I can't remember due to how much I had to drink at the time, even those were nothing more than fun-fuelled interactions with no risk of anybody being hurt.

'The big thing is motive,' Nicola said to me as we tried to come up with one name from my past who could have an axe to grind. 'It's not so much who would want to do something like this, but why.'

I'd put a lot of thought into that, but had failed to land on any solid motive that somebody might have for potentially murdering every man I have ever been in a relationship with.

'I can't think of anybody I might have hurt,' I say, shaking my head. 'Other than Shaun and Calum when I broke up with them, but it's obviously not them because they're dead.'

'What if it's not about revenge?' Nicola suggests.

'What do you mean?'

'What if it's about something else? Like jealousy, perhaps.'

'You think somebody is jealous of me?'

'Maybe. Or they are jealous of the people who have been with you, which might explain why they would want to take them all out.'

I think about that for a second but quickly stop when the thought of my fiancé pops into my mind. The way he gets tetchy whenever I bring up the subject of one of my exes. The fact that I know he feels uncomfortable about me having had more sexual partners than he has. And the fact that he reacted with disdain when I floated this theory of a potential serial killer with him earlier.

But I'm being silly. Tom isn't behind this. He's one of the people in danger, not the person perpetrating it.

'I don't know who would be jealous of me,' I say, leaning my elbows against the table and resting my head in my hands. The alcohol is starting to make me feel a little fuzzy, and I have a feeling that getting up from my seat won't be fun when I eventually give it a try.

'Is there anybody who might have asked you out

over the years, and you turned them down?' Nicola asks.

'Well, yeah, there's been a few. But I was always polite to anybody I rejected because I always thought it took balls to put yourself out there like that.'

'That might not make a difference. Even if you were polite, somebody could still be jealous if they see you with another guy they think could have been them.'

I know Nicola is making valid points, but I'm almost starting to wish she wasn't. The more she says, the more she is giving me to worry about. I'm having a hard enough time trying to come up with a figure from my past that might have a reason to feel like I mistreated them, without having to try to recall every single person who may or may not have shown some interest in me over the years.

'I mean, how deep do we have to go here?' I ask. 'A guy once asked me out when I was on the bus into town. Is he a suspect now?'

'I don't know.'

'What about the old man who asked me to go for a drink with him as we stood in the queue at the post office four years ago? Is he a suspect, or is he dead now, so we can rule him out?'

Nicola apparently picks up on my sarcastic under-tones because she shrugs her shoulders and sits back in her seat as if to say that she doesn't have to offer any more suggestions if I don't want them.

'I'm sorry,' I tell her before reaching for the wine bottle again and offering the dregs to her as some kind of goodwill gesture.

'I'm just trying to help,' she says before nodding her head and accepting the last bit of wine like I knew she would.

'I know you are. The problem is that it shouldn't be you trying to help me. It should be the police.'

'They said they would look into Shaun's death, didn't they?'

'Yeah, but how long will that take? Meanwhile, my other exes are still at risk, never mind my fiancé.'

'Who did you say was next in line?' Nicola asks me as she sits forward, seemingly happy to offer her assistance again after our brief bit of tension.

'Ash. He was my boyfriend after Ryan.'

'Okay, and the police said they wouldn't send somebody to look after him until they knew for certain that something was wrong?'

'Yeah,' I reply, nodding my head. 'But that's the problem. He might be dead before they know that. I wanted them to contact him at least and give him a warning, but they wouldn't.'

'Well, if they won't do it, why can't you?'

Nicola's question is a good one, but while it seems it might have an obvious answer, it's actually a rather complicated one.

'I'd rather not get in touch with him myself if I can help it.'

'Why? You just said you think he could be the next one to die.'

'Yeah, but it's not that simple. I can't just message him out of the blue and tell him he might be the victim of an apparent accident sometime soon.'

'Why not? I presume you have him on social media, right?'

I nod.

'Then just drop him a quick message and tell him to be careful,' Nicola says, making it sound as easy as that.

But it's not. For starters, I don't want to be reaching out to any of my exes regardless of what the topic of conversation might be. I know that doing such a thing is only likely to irritate Tom even more and make him feel worse about the state of our relationship right now. But I don't want to say this to Nicola because then she will think I'm getting married to a guy who doesn't trust me, which is not the case.

'What is it? What's the problem with sending him a message?' she asks me after I have failed to come back with a good response.

'It's nothing. It's just I shouldn't be messaging old boyfriends.'

'Why not? Because you're with Tom now? So what? He doesn't have to know, and it's not as if you're doing anything seedy behind his back. You're trying to save their life, not hook up with them.'

'I just hate keeping secrets from him.'

'Then tell him. But you have to do something, don't you? How would you feel if you did nothing and then Ash turns up dead? You'd wished you'd warned him then, wouldn't you?'

Nicola is right. I would feel guilty. I guess it wouldn't do any harm for me to give him a heads-up, just to be on the lookout for anything that might represent danger.

'Fine. I'll message him,' I say, taking my phone from my handbag and tapping on the app belonging to the social media platform where I know Ash is most active these days. 'I just have to try not to sound crazy. Maybe something like hi, Ash, all my exes have started dying, so please be careful, as I'm worried you might be next.'

I'm being sarcastic again, but Nicola either doesn't pick up on it or chooses to ignore it.

'I think you're doing the right thing,' Nicola tells me as I type, giving me the final bit of encouragement before I finish and press Send.

'Done,' I say, putting my phone down on the table.

'Which one was Ash again?' Nicola asks, so I show her his profile photo online. 'Oh, right, yeah. I remember him. The hottie.'

I laugh as I snatch my phone back and put it somewhere more secure, where she can't look at it again. Then I check the time and decide that I'd better get going because it's getting late, and once again, Tom has no idea where I am. The fact he hasn't tried to call me since I left the house suggests he is still mad at me, and I expect another argument when I get home. I won't mention my message to Ash to him when we do speak. The mention of my ex will only annoy Tom even more, but I'm trying to help Ash as well as save Tom from any harm in the future. If Ash gets hurt, that only leaves my last ex, Jesse, standing between a potential killer and my fiancé. If I can protect Ash, I can protect Tom down the line.

I'll just have to hope that I'm wrong about all of this, and Ash ends up being fine, meaning there really isn't a serial killer working their way through my old flames. But that mysterious message is still on my phone, and the fact that it exists tells me something I don't want to know.

Ash is in trouble.

I just hope he takes my message seriously.

## 18

T he taxi I'm in is about five minutes away from my house when I see the message from Ash pop up on my phone. It only takes me five seconds to read it and a further second to realise that I might have made a mistake in contacting him.

*Hey, stranger. Long time no speak. How's things? What's all this about me being in danger? Have you been drinking tonight? If so, you're not the only one. What else is on your mind? xx*

Ash was always the flirty type, and it sounds as if he hasn't changed. Not even an ominous message from me about a potential risk to his life is enough to stop him from being suggestive. But I wish he'd replied more sensibly, as well as a little less cheekily, and not just because I'm trying to give him a warning that he needs to listen to. It's also because I know that like me, he is engaged to be married, so I'd be much more comfortable without the kisses and the question about what else is on my mind, as if there is any doubt what is on his.

I know exactly what he is thinking about because it'll be the same thing that he spent most of our relationship thinking about too.

Other women.

I met Ash when I started working at a local accountancy company in the town centre a few months after I returned home from my extensive travels. Back then, I was having a hard time settling back into the drudgery of the 'real world' as it was, and my low mood wasn't helped by the permanent dark clouds that seemed to hover over my hometown as winter kicked in and blue skies became a distant memory. At that time, as I finally entered the working world at the fairly senior age of twenty-six, I was looking for anything that could cheer me up and brighten my days.

Ash turned out to be that thing.

I spotted him when I was being shown around the office on my first day, doing my best to remember the overwhelming number of names I was being given as I shook several hands and smiled at all the unfamiliar faces. He was standing by the printer, wearing a smart blue suit and looking much happier than most of the other people in the office, who all seemed to be overweight, fed up, or both. By the time I was introduced to him, I was already feeling a little nervous and wanted to do my best to make a good first impression, even though I doubted anything was ever going to come of it. He looked to be a few years older than I was, somewhere around his mid-thirties, so I presumed I would be too young for him.

But I was wrong.

It was clear from day one that he was just as attracted to me as I was to him, and it only took a couple of weeks and one after-work drinks session to do something about it. We kissed outside the pub that the rest of

our colleagues were drinking in, and that was the beginning of what became an exciting but ultimately tumul-
tuous relationship. Ash would wine and dine me, he
would take me on lavish shopping sprees, and he would
never hesitate to book us into an expensive hotel room
every few weeks, giving me a taste of the kind of lifestyle that the previous men in my life hadn't been able
to do. The fact that he was almost ten years older than
me meant that he had way more money than I did,
having been an accountant for most of his life, while I
was blowing what little money I had at uni or abroad.
But I wasn't with him for the money, although we
certainly enjoyed it. I was with him because he made me
feel good and showed me that moving back home and
settling down didn't have to be as boring as I had feared
it would be. But in hindsight, the warning signs were
there early. Like how it took him forever to let me stay
overnight at his place when we were dating, instead
preferring my place or even hotels, as well as many
excuses that he simply wanted to get a good night's
sleep by himself. Or like how he would sometimes take
hours to text me back, making me wonder what he was
up to when he had led me to believe that he was just
home alone.

In the end, I found out what he was up to.

He was in a relationship, and he had been in one
ever since we had met.

Of course, I ended things with him as soon as I
found out, mortified that I was technically 'the other
woman' and afraid that his partner would find out
about me and accuse me of being some kind of home-
wrecker. But Ash apologised for the deceit and told me
that he had been planning to leave his current partner
and be with me but had been struggling to pluck up the

courage to do so. I should have walked away then. It would have saved me a couple of years and a broken heart. But stupidly, I gave him a choice. Her or me.

He chose me.

Naively, I thought that meant there would be no more future obstacles to have to navigate, and I felt excited on the day that we were able to move into our own place together. I shared photos of the two of us on social media in our new home as we decorated the Christmas tree or had friends over for a barbecue in the summer, feeling like I was finally grown up and settled, and it was only a matter of time until I had a ring on my finger to prove it. I even ignored the note of caution from Nicola at the time, who had warned me that if Ash had been capable of seeing two women at the same time when he met me, he was capable of doing it again. But I disagreed. I said Ash had changed and that I was different from his last girlfriend.

I was wrong. It was one week after my twenty-eighth birthday when I found out that Ash was messaging other women. He'd left his phone at home by mistake one day when he had gone to the shops to get us breakfast, and while I felt bad for snooping, I had a look, as if to prove to myself that Nicola was wrong. But she was right. He was up to his old tricks again, and he had been lying to me.

I confronted him when he got back. We argued. He apologised. I almost felt like accepting it, if only because I didn't want to have to start all over again when it came to love. But in the end, I had to go. I packed my bags and moved back home with my parents, feeling like a failure and still no nearer to finding the man whom I would spend the rest of my life with.

That was eight years ago, and a lot has changed

since then. But it seems like Ash hasn't. He's in his forties now, but that seems to have done nothing to have slowed down his sex drive because no sooner has my taxi pulled up outside my house than he has sent me a second message.

*How's your wedding planning going? Are you as bored with it all as I am? Haha. Wanna do a video chat? Xx*

I pay the taxi driver and allow him to get on his way before turning to look at my house and wondering if Tom is still up. All the lights are off inside, so I'm guessing not, although maybe he has gone out too and I'm the first one home. I think about how I'd quite like that because that would mean I wouldn't have to face a potential argument when I walk in. But I'd also be sad if he has gone out without telling me, and it surely isn't a good sign if we've both taken to doing our own thing without letting the other one know where we are. But there's only one way to find out, so I head up the driveway and unlock the front door, ready to discover if I'm home alone or home in time for another fight.

It turns out that it's neither.

I discover Tom lying in bed, asleep or at least pretending to be, and it's a relief because I don't have to worry about where he might be, nor about the fact that we might have another heated exchange of words.

Doing my best to get undressed as quietly as possible, I eventually get under the duvet beside him and prepare to get some sleep of my own until I notice that I have another notification on my screen from Ash.

It's a missed video call.

He really has been drinking tonight.

I decide to nip this in the bud now and send him a

quick message back, telling him to be careful but not to message me anymore. Then I leave it at that, putting my phone on the bedside table and closing my eyes.

After a busy and stressful day, sleep comes mercifully quickly for me.

## 19

I wake up to the sounds of Tom getting dressed. Unlike me last night, he seems to be making no attempt to be as quiet as possible. I get confirmation of that when he walks into our en-suite bathroom and shuts the door loudly before I hear his electric toothbrush go on, followed by more crashing and banging about seconds later.

I guess him being asleep when I got home last night was only delaying the inevitable. He's still mad at me after I left and went to the police station, and he's making it known by waking me up while he gets ready for work. Usually, he creeps about because he knows that I don't have to get up anywhere near as early as he does on a weekday, but no such luck now.

Today, he doesn't seem to give a damn about me.

I sigh and think about getting up and facing reality when I decide to put it off for a few moments longer by picking up my phone and seeing what distractions I can lose myself in there. But a quick glance at my screen gives me the kind of distraction I don't need.

There is another message on there from Ash, which

must have been sent after I had already fallen asleep. But even with my phone locked, it's possible to read all of it because it's only short.

*Good to hear from you tonight, stranger. Let's get a drink soon and toast to the old times. xx*

I feel sick, but it has nothing to do with the content of Ash's message. Rather, it's because I wonder if Tom saw this message on my phone when he woke up this morning. I wonder if that is why he is being so moody now.

It could just be the paranoia from consuming the best part of two bottles of wine last night, but as I pull back the duvet and put my feet onto the carpet, I feel as if I have somehow been found guilty of doing something I shouldn't have. But I haven't done anything wrong. I only messaged Ash to warn him. I didn't know he was going to send me messages harking back to the old times, and I certainly didn't expect him to put kisses at the end of them.

There were definitely no kisses in mine.

Now I'm afraid that Tom has seen the message and thinks I'm up to something behind his back, although I know there is only one way that I can alleviate that fear.

I need to ask him.

Reaching the door to the bathroom, I knock a couple of times, although I doubt that he has heard me over all the noise he is making on the other side. I have no choice but to wait for him to finish up in there and come out, where I'll be able to see him and get a better idea of what he is really thinking right now.

After a few more minutes alone with my paranoia, I hear him turn off his toothbrush, flush the toilet, and unlock the bathroom door. I step away from it as it opens and see the look on his face when he spots me waiting for him.

'Hey,' I say, trying not to be too chirpy because I know that everything isn't all right between us but also trying not to be too downbeat because I don't want him to think that I have anything to hide.

'Hey,' he offers back before walking past me and opening the wardrobe, where he takes out a red tie and puts it around his neck.

He looks as if he is just getting ready for work like it's a normal day, but I know it isn't. We aren't usually this awkward around each other.

'I'm sorry for yesterday,' I say, taking a step towards him as he knots his tie.

'Me too,' he replies, not taking his eyes off the mirror in front of him.

'I went out for a few drinks with Nicola after the police station. I should have called you but—'

'It's fine. I guessed that's what you were up to.'

I feel bad, and not just because I'm obviously so predictable. It's also because I realise my answer to all our disagreements is usually for me to go out drinking with my friend instead of being here to sort it out with the man I am marrying.

'So you still went to the police, did you?' he asks as he pulls off his tie and throws it back into the wardrobe before taking out a blue one instead.

'Yeah. I wanted to see if they thought there was anything to worry about.'

'And?'

'They are going to look into a few things,' I reply, although my tone of voice must give away how unconfident I am about them being able to find anything because Tom shrugs and says nothing more about it.

While I'm glad he seems to have lost the energy to

argue with me about my concerns of a potential serial killer working their way through my former lovers, I still have a gnawing sense of dread in the pit of my stomach. I still don't know if he saw the message from Ash on my phone when he got up before me this morning. If he did, he obviously isn't going to make it apparent without me asking him.

I realise I could say nothing, assume he didn't see it, and hope for the best. But the fear that he might have seen it makes me anxious because if he has seen it, then he might be thinking that I'm up to something behind his back. I'd hate that because not only do I love him, but I'd never cheat on him, so the fact that he might think I would is a dreadful one.

I've got no choice unless I want to go all day worrying about it.

I'm just going to have to bring it up myself.

'I messaged one of my exes yesterday,' I say, taking the bull by the horns. 'A guy called Ash. You probably remember I told you about him. If I'm right about this, then he is in danger now.'

Tom pauses for a moment before continuing to fasten his tie.

'I hope you don't mind me doing that,' I go on nervously. 'I haven't messaged him for years, not since we broke up. But I just felt like I should warn him, just in case.'

'Just in case,' Tom says with a chuckle, though it's so quiet that it's more for himself than for me.

I can't tell if he's being like this because he did see the message or because he is annoyed that I just told him I'd been in touch with an ex, so I press on.

'But I kind of wish I hadn't done now because he's been messaging me a few times since then, and now he wants to go for a drink. But obviously I'm not going to go. I don't want to see him again. I just wanted to tell him to be careful.'

Tom says nothing.

'He's getting married soon too,' I add as if to reinforce the fact that any affair between the two of us is even more unlikely now we are both engaged, although I know that as far as Ash is concerned, that means very little.

'Here we go again, you and your exes,' Tom finally says when he has finished with his new tie and pulled on his suit jacket. 'I'm sick of hearing about them, if I'm honest. If it's not Shaun, it's Ash or Ryan or some guy from uni.'

'Tom, I—'

'Just leave it. I don't want to hear any more apologies or excuses or wild theories about serial killers murdering all the men you used to date. All I want is for you to go back to being the woman I proposed to.'

'Tom, you know I love you. I just—'

But Tom isn't listening anymore. He's already left the bedroom and is making his way down the stairs, where I know he will only be a few seconds away from grabbing his car keys, walking out the front door, and driving away. I could run after him and make him stop, telling him that I'm sorry, that I've been stupid to dredge up all this history about my exes and that I need to stop speculating about some serial killer coming for the men I used to love. But I don't. Instead, I stay in the bedroom as I hear the front door slam shut and the car engine start on the driveway outside. I stay there because – despite how much I love him and how much I want to prove it – I know I can't apologise for my behaviour recently. Certainly not for yesterday when I went to the police station or when I messaged Ash to warn him about a potential killer going after him.

I have nothing to apologise for.

Despite what Tom thinks, and despite what I wish were the case, I know there is something going on.

I know that the deaths aren't going to stop.

Not yet.

Not when the message told me that there's still three to go.

## 20

Maybe I should have just stayed in bed and not got up to have the talk with Tom. That way, I'd probably still be under the duvet now instead of sitting in this stifling sauna, trying to sweat out my hangover before I go into the office for a full day's work.

I've never been one to go to the gym first thing in the morning, mainly because I'm never up and out of bed in time. But with little chance of a lie-in after Tom's loud behaviour in our bedroom woke me, I decided that I would try to make the most of it by getting in a work-out. Sadly, like most things I have done recently, it seems to have been a bad idea.

I lasted all of five minutes in the gym before retreating into the changing rooms, pulling off my shorts and T-shirt, and swapping them out for my swimsuit and towel. Then I headed into the sauna, where I have been sitting ever since. I had hoped that the high temperature would cleanse my pores and make me feel refreshed after so much wine last night, but if anything, I feel worse for being here. I know I should just get out and quit while I'm behind, but I'm stubborn as well as stupid, so I'm trying my best not to give in until I have to.

As I sit in the steamy room, barely able to see more than a few inches in front of my face, I think about Ash and whether or not he has paid any attention to the warning I sent him. Based on his responses, he seemed more bothered about rekindling any potential romance with me rather than looking over his shoulder and making sure that he was safe, so I'm not hopeful that my warning has been heeded. Nor do I feel as if any guilt I might have about him being a target has been assuaged, even though I think I have done everything I can to hopefully keep him safe. The truth is that unless the police find anything suspicious, and unless everybody I warn takes me seriously, then nothing is going to change. That means it's only a matter of time until Ash winds up dead, and that makes me feel sick because he doesn't deserve to die, just like those before him didn't deserve to die either.

I just wonder what the form of 'accident' will be this time. A slip, trip, or fall at home, perhaps, causing him to tumble down his stairs and break his neck. Or maybe an issue with a 'faulty' gas pipe could result in a fireball ripping through his house and taking him out in a blazing inferno, not too dissimilar to how Ryan died. Whatever it is, I feel like the police are not going to treat it any differently to any of the other deaths unless they know for sure that somebody caused it to happen on purpose.

But will that happen? Will the killer make a mistake and leave a clue? Or will they make it look like murder for a change, perhaps because they want me to know for certain that they are coming for every one of my lovers, and there's nothing I can do about it?

Maybe it's the heat, or just my hangover, but I suddenly feel sick and need to get out of here. Getting up from the dry bench, I rush forwards in the direction of the glass door where I entered, and while I can't see it because of all the steam, I'm putting my faith in my memory.

Fortunately, I'm right, and my hand touches the surface of the door before I'm able to find the handle and use it to get out of the scorching sauna. As soon as the door is open, I feel the relief of the cool air hitting my body, as well as feeling a little better about all the worries that were racing through my mind a few minutes ago. I'm aware that while things are bad, they probably seem a lot worse because of the tired and dehydrated state my body seems to always be in these days, thanks to all the drinking I'm doing. Maybe things wouldn't look so bleak if I just had some early nights and kept a clear head. With that in mind, I make a promise to myself that I am not going to drink again until this is all over.

I'm on my way back to the changing rooms when I glance at the large swimming pool to my left and notice that it is completely empty. I've never been a big swimmer, but at that moment, the water looks extremely inviting, and I decide that I have five minutes to spare to slide beneath the surface and get some movement into my bones.

Sitting down on the edge of the pool, the cool water feels good on my hot skin, and the further I slide in, the better I start to feel about things. A minute later, I'm swimming as fast as I can towards the other end, breast-stroke, though I'm keeping my head firmly above water so as not to get chlorine in my eyes. The last thing I want is to turn up at work with red eyes.

It's only when I reach the other end and turn around

to go back that I notice that I'm no longer alone in the pool. Somebody else has got in here while my back was turned, and while that wouldn't necessarily be a problem, it is when I spot the person swimming towards me.

It's the creepy guy from the gym, the one who is always watching me.

*Peter The Pervert.*

I look around the edge of the pool for the ladders, but they're at the other end. The only way out down here is to pull myself up onto the side, but that won't be easy. I doubt I have the arm strength to do that, plus I'm in the deep end, so I can't use the bottom of the pool to propel me up either. The only thing I can do is try to swim past the guy before he gets to this end. That way, I should be able to avoid any awkward feelings that will undoubtedly occur should he end up bobbing in the water beside me.

I move to the opposite side of the pool to the one he is swimming towards me in and then push my legs against the wall, using the momentum to pick up speed quickly as I begin to swim as fast as I can towards the other end. I'm about halfway there when the man suddenly turns off course and begins heading straight at me, his head above the water and his eyes on me like they always are.

I have no idea what he's doing, but I don't want to hang around to find out, so I keep swimming, my sights firmly on the ladder ahead. But the man is faster than I am, and he is closing the gap quickly, leaving me to realise that there is no way I will be able to make it out of here before he gets to me.

I look over my shoulder and see him advancing through the water, a disturbingly calm look on his face as he stares right at me. I begin to panic and lose my rhythm, causing my speed to slow and the gap between us to close even quicker now.

What is he doing? What does he want?

Like it or not, I feel like I'm about to find out. Reaching out for the wall beside me, I grab onto it and prepare to kick out at him if he gets any closer, not that the determination on his face suggests that will make much of a difference in his desire to get near. But just before he reaches me, the door to the changing rooms opens, and two men walk in, their bulging stomachs on show in their skimpy pair of Speedos.

The sudden arrival of the two men causes the man in the pool to stop swimming towards me, and he turns away, gliding through the water towards the other end of the pool and leaving me alone.

I have no idea what he was going to do when he caught up to me, but I'm grateful that I don't have to find out. Swimming quickly over to the ladders, I pull myself out of the water and grab my towel from the bench before hurrying away into the changing rooms, not even looking back over my shoulder as I go.

It's only when I'm in the sanctuary of the female-only rooms that I have a thought.

What if the creepy man in the pool is the person behind the text message?

What if he is the one who has been targeting my exes?

## 21

I've got changed without showering beforehand, and now I'm making my way to the reception desk in the gym, where I hope to be able to find out the name of the man who made me feel so uncomfortable in the swimming pool. But I'm not going to find out just so I can make a complaint about him to the staff here.

I'm doing it so I can hopefully have a name to pass on to the police as a potential suspect.

I hurry through the busy café area, which is always full of people who seem to spend more time here drinking coffee than they do exercising on the gym floor, but I know I shouldn't judge them. I'm not a stranger to that type of behaviour, and I'd actually kill for a coffee right now. But first, I need to speak to the receptionist.

'Hi, I'm wondering if you can help me?' I say as I reach the front desk and lean my elbows against it, noticing the array of leaflets about exercise classes and personal training goals scattered about beside me.

The bored young woman behind the desk puts on her best fake smile to let me know that she would like to help me but only because she is being paid to do so.

'I was in the pool about fifteen minutes ago, and there was a man in there who I've seen here before. He's always been watching me whenever I exercise, but today in the pool, he started swimming directly towards me, and it made me feel very uncomfortable.'

'Oh,' the receptionist says, glancing nervously towards the office behind her to where I presume her manager is sitting. She was probably expecting a query about a spin class or a complaint about a broken piece of equipment, not an accusation of one of the members being a creep.

'I was just wondering if you could find out who he is by checking the cameras?'

'You want to make a complaint against him?'

'Yes,' I say, deciding that's a better thing to do rather than admit that I'm actually hoping to be able to pass on this man's name to the police to see if he is in any way connected to the deaths of my three ex-boyfriends.

'Okay, just one second,' the receptionist says, and she scurries away into the office, where I can see her talking to the bearded man sitting at a computer. He looks at me a few seconds later before getting up and walking over, no doubt concerned that he might be about to lose a paying member if he doesn't resolve this issue quickly.

'Hi, how can I help you?' he says as he reaches me, and I sigh before preparing to say exactly what I just said to the receptionist again when I notice the doors to the men's changing room open and the guy from the pool walking out.

'Wait, that's him!' I say, pointing towards the guy entering the café with a rucksack slung over his shoulder.

I'm expecting the receptionist or her manager to do something productive with that information, like go and have a word with him or at least give me some kind of form to fill in, but they don't do that. Instead, they both share an uneasy look with each other before the manager speaks.

'His name is David. He's one of our members on our Inclusive Fitness Initiative Scheme.'

I have no idea what that means, and my face must make that clear because the manager quickly continues.

'He has a mental disability, and it affects how he interacts with others,' he goes on. 'That's his carer over there. She waits for him in the café while he exercises.'

That's when I see the man taking a seat at a table opposite a middle-aged woman with a cappuccino. She smiles at David, and only now I watch him properly do I see that he is extremely awkward socially and avoids eye contact with the woman he is talking to.

'I'll have a word with her and ask her to tell David not to bother you anymore,' the manager says, which only makes me feel guilty. 'This has happened with a couple of our members before, and we have warned him. He's harmless, but if he's made you feel uncomfortable, then you're right to bring it up, and we can ask him to leave you alone.'

I feel my face flushing red. All this time, I thought David was just some pervert in the gym. Now I feel terrible.

'No, that's okay. Don't say anything,' I tell the manager, shaking my head.

'Are you sure?'

'Yeah, absolutely,' I confirm before smiling and walking away from the desk.

I decide to quit while I'm behind and leave the gym as fast as I can, not wishing to hang around where presumably the manager and the receptionist are thinking how bad a person I am for wanting to report somebody with a disability. It's not my fault for feeling uncomfortable in the pool, but it's also not his fault either. I also don't want them to see how embarrassed I am for thinking I had some kind of stalker when there was a more innocent explanation.

Pushing through the glass doors that lead me back into the car park, I feel better for being out in the fresh air, but I'm not entirely comfortable until I make it back to my car and slam the door shut. Letting out a deep breath as I lean against my steering wheel, I cringe at the awkward situation I just found myself in, and my mood isn't helped when I see David and his carer leaving the gym a few minutes later.

I watch them as they walk hand in hand across the car park, and now I see what the manager was saying. David really is harmless.

After watching David and his carer drive away, I decide that I need to get a move on too, so I put my car into motion and set off in the direction of my office. I'm due to start work in twenty minutes, although in my tired, embarrassed, and stressed-out state, the last thing I need now is eight hours scouring through spreadsheets full of numbers and equations. I don't mind being an accountant, but it's not the easiest job in the world to do at the best of times, never mind the day after wine, a bad night's sleep and an eventful morning in the gym swimming pool.

I need something to take my mind off my worries, so I turn the radio on and go in search of an upbeat song to lift my mood. But it's eight thirty, which means all the stations are currently broadcasting the breakfast news, so I give up and leave one of the stations on as I continue driving.

It's as I'm approaching a set of traffic lights near my office when I hear the reporter on the radio mention a name that almost causes me to slam on the brakes.

*"The family of Shaun Gibson are said to be shocked and saddened by the rumours circulating online about his death. The thirty-six-year-old's body was found in Billinge Wood just over a fortnight ago, and police said there were no suspicious circumstances surrounding the death at the time. But several posts on social media overnight have caused his family great distress after some users discussed the possibility that he was murdered. But the police have stressed that there is no evidence to suggest that and have warned anybody using social media to spread fake and hurtful rumours that they can and will be punished by the law."*

I stare at my car radio as if I can get any answers by doing so, but the news bulletin ends and is quickly replaced by a pop song that does not fit the mood that I'm in. Quickly turning the music off, I think about what I just heard and wonder how it could be possible. I hadn't noticed anything online about Shaun's death recently, although I haven't checked social media since yesterday morning. But I'm the only one who thinks there was more to it than suicide. Unless somebody else thinks it too.

But who?

It's only when I get to the office car park and check my mobile that I start to get a better idea of what happened. I see a post on social media from a woman called Karen, who used to be one of my classmates at school. We're just Facebook friends now rather than real-life ones, although I do know Nicola still sees her from time to time. It's only after reading Karen's post that I realise it's that relationship that has caused all of this drama on the radio.

Karen has been spreading the rumours about Shaun's death, and she has admitted where she got the idea from.

*Me.*

My breath catches in my throat as I realise my name has been used in connection with the rumours surrounding Shaun's suicide potentially being a murder. But there is only a couple of ways that could be possible. Either someone in the police has leaked what I told them, or Nicola has relayed our private conversation to Karen, who in turn went online and shared it with the world.

I can't believe a police officer would have been this irresponsible, but I also can't believe that my best friend could have been gossiping about me. I told her about my worries and suspicions in confidence, and it meant a lot that I thought she believed me. But I hadn't expected her to talk about it with other people.

Then the tsunami of notifications start. I don't want to look at them, but I can't help it. Going onto my profile page, I see that I am starting to get all sorts of abuse from other users, in particular several members of Shaun's family.

This is a disaster.

What am I supposed to do? What can I do? I need to ask Nicola if this is her, but what if it isn't? I don't want to lose one of the few good friends I have these days.

I don't know what to do as the notifications keep coming, except I feel like throwing my phone out of the car window.

Maybe it's best if I just delete my social media accounts. But that's a short-term strategy and won't do me much good in the long term. It won't do me much good now that I might be the most hated woman in town.

## 22

I t turns out that those first few seconds when I woke up this morning were the best part of my day. Everything went south very quickly after that with my argument with Tom, my embarrassment at the gym, and then the fact that I was being accused of spreading fake rumours about a popular man's death. Add in the fact that work was busier than usual, I spilt coffee all over myself on my lunch hour, and I have another migraine from my teenage accident, and it's safe to say that by the time I got home, I was ready to scream.

Is it any wonder I've been sitting on the living room floor for the last three hours, pouring myself extremely generous servings of vodka and lemonade, and doing everything I can to forget about how many people have been hurt because of their connection to me?

I'm alone because Tom isn't home yet, not that his presence would make things much better considering how things have been between us recently. But my isolation is also down to the fact that I have refused to answer any calls from Nicola since she has been trying to reach me tonight. She might be wanting to apologise for talking about my private life with Karen and causing not only social media to explode, but for the police to have to come out and make a statement on a grieving family's behalf. Maybe I should give her a chance to defend herself, and maybe it wasn't even her who leaked it, but I just want to be left alone right now. I haven't answered her calls because I don't want to speak to her, but not just because I feel betrayed. A consequence of her actions is that the police have made it perfectly clear that they are not taking my concerns seriously. There I was thinking that PC Brown and his colleagues were diligently looking into the text message I received, as well as the fact that Shaun may very well have been murdered, yet their statement today makes it clear that they either haven't looked into it at all or have found nothing and moved on.

So where does that leave me?

And what does it mean for the rest of my exes and, most importantly, Tom?

I'm drunk, but I'm a long way from calling it a night. I might even just sleep down here on the sofa. Tom would be alarmed to find me like that, but maybe then he might start to take me seriously and believe me when I say that something is wrong.

But what if it isn't?

Even after everything that has happened today, that thought is the thing that is causing me to feel the lowest. If I have been wrong about all of this and there is nothing sinister going on with my ex-boyfriends, then this has been a costly mistake. My relationship with Tom is strained for the first time ever. So too, my relationship with Nicola. And to top it all off, I'm being named and shamed on social media.

Is it any wonder I'm hitting the vodka like there's no tomorrow?

I'm just about to take another sip when I hear my phone vibrating on the carpet beside me. I almost don't bother to look at it because I expect it'll just be Nicola calling again and hoping to apologise to me. But I check on it, and to my surprise, it's not her. Nor is it Tom, who would have been the other candidate I would have expected to try to get in touch with me.

It's Ash.

I stare at his name on my phone's screen as it keeps ringing, trying to figure out if it would be a good idea to answer it or not. Not only is my ex calling me, but it's also half-past ten at night. There can only be one good reason for him to be calling me this late.

He must have been drinking too.

Against my better judgement, I accept the call, putting the phone to my ear and saying hello.

Immediately, I can tell that Ash is outside somewhere. The sound of the wind blowing around the phone, as well as the noise of several vehicles passing him by on the road, is proof of that. I wonder where he is and what he is doing. But he's not the only one with questions on his mind.

'Hey! What you up to?' he asks me enthusiastically.

'I'm at home. Why are you calling me?' I reply, not wishing to encourage him.

'I was seeing if you wanted to come out for a drink!'

As I suspected, Ash is drunk. There are numerous giveaways and not just the fact that he has asked me to go for a drink with him. There's the loud volume of his voice and the fact that he slurred the end of his sentence.

'No, I'm fine, thanks,' I say, preparing to hang up. 'You shouldn't be calling me.'

'You shouldn't have texted me the other day, then,'

he replies, referring to the message I sent him, telling him to be careful. 'You were obviously thinking about me. Well, guess what, now I'm thinking about you.'

He hasn't changed since I dated him several years ago. He's cheeky, flirty, and acting as if he is single, which he most definitely is not.

'Ash, you're drunk. Go home and be with your fiancée,' I tell him as if I'm some wise old sage who knows what's best for other people. But the fact that I'm currently sitting home alone drinking stupid amounts of vodka while my fiancé is out somewhere suggests that I don't know anything.

'But I want to be with you.'

'Don't say that.'

'Why not? It's the truth. Do you ever think about us two?'

'No, and you shouldn't think about us either.'

'Liar. You wouldn't have answered my call if you didn't care.'

I want to hang up, but he makes a point. If there wasn't some part of me that was seeking a little company, then why did I answer? I can pretend all I want about it being because I want to make sure he is safe from any potential serial killer targeting my exes, but is it really? Or am I talking to him because I want to feel like somebody wants me?

'Do you want me to come around to yours?' he asks me as what sounds like a bus drives past him loudly.

'No, I do not!' I reply firmly before asking him where he is in case he is only around the corner. If he is, then I would need to go and lock the door quickly. The last thing I need is Tom getting home and finding one of my exes standing on the doorstep or, worse, in the house.

'I'm in town. I've just been to the Swan,' he tells me, and I know which pub he means because Nicola and I have spent many a night in there before. It's a small pub, but what it lacks in size, it more than makes up for in cheap drinks and a sociable atmosphere. Part of me wishes I had been in there tonight because it would surely have been better than drinking by myself on the floor of an empty house.

'Are you coming out?' Ash asks me again.

'No, I'm not. And I'm hanging up now.'

'Wait, don't do that!'

'Why not?'

'Don't you want to make sure I get home safe?'

I roll my eyes.

'I'm sure you'll be fine,' I tell him, and I hear the noise levels around him drop, suggesting he has left the busy town centre street behind and is now walking along a much quieter one.

'I don't know about that. Someone has been following me ever since I left the pub, and they're still behind me now.'

Ash chuckles at the other end of the line, but I'm not laughing.

'Who is it?' I ask him, suddenly worried for his safety.

'I don't know. They've got a cap on. Can't really see their face. But they are definitely following me.'

Ash's voice doesn't carry much concern, but I'm going to have to change that because if I'm right, then something is wrong.

'Ash, you need to be careful. They might be dangerous.'

'What are you talking about?'

'Three of my ex-boyfriends have died recently, and I think you might be next. That's why I messaged you the other day. Please, you need to be careful!'

'Slow down. You're not making any sense.'

'Ash, listen to me. I think you might be in danger.'

'Who is this? They're definitely getting closer.'

'Ash!'

I listen, but it all goes quiet for a few seconds until I fear the worst.

'Ash! Are you there?'

Nothing.

The only thing I can hear is the sound of my own heart hammering inside me.

Until... laughter.

'Don't worry, they turned off. They mustn't have been following me after all,' Ash says, sounding nowhere near as stressed as I have just been.

'Are you sure?' I ask him, taking a few deep breaths to try to calm myself down.

'Yep, positive. They're gone. It's just me now. All alone. Want to come and keep me company?'

I relax again. If he's back to his flirty self, then there must be nothing to worry about.

'I'm going now. And don't call me again,' I say before hanging up.

I put the phone back down on the carpet and pick up my drink, feeling like I need it after that dramatic moment on the call.

The buzzing of my phone again lets me know that Ash is trying to get me back on the line, but I don't answer it this time. Instead, I just finish my drink, rest my head on a cushion from the sofa and close my eyes.

## 23

I wake up to bright sunlight streaming through the open window opposite me, and it takes me a few seconds to work out where I am. I'm in the living room, curled up on the carpet with a cushion covered in drool. Oh, god, I fell asleep down here.

What the hell must Tom think of me?

I reach out for my phone to give me some idea of what time it is, but the battery is dead, so I don't know if it's dawn or if I've overslept and the working day has already begun. Feeling remorseful for several reasons, I force myself to my feet and head for the door, praying that Tom is upstairs in bed because at least that will mean it's still early. If he has left, then it literally could be any time, and I might have some serious explaining to do with my boss.

Heading up the stairs, I lose my balance halfway up and bump into the wall, and that's when I realise that I'm still drunk from last night. It's been a long time since I had to go through the process of sobering up before the hangover kicked in, but then I did have a lot of vodka last night. At least I don't feel as bad yet as I surely will in a few hours' time.

The bedroom door is closed, but that gives me no clue as to if Tom is inside or has already left, so I enter the bedroom and look nervously towards the bed.

He's not there.

The bed is slept in, but it's empty.

Oh no, he's been and gone, and I spent the whole time sleeping downstairs beside a bottle of vodka. What the hell will he think of me?

'Good morning.'

The sound of his voice to my left almost makes me jump out of my skin, and I turn to see him standing in the en-suite with his toothbrush in his hand.

'Tom! I thought you'd already left!'

'It's only ten past six,' he says before sticking the brush in his mouth and scrubbing.

It's a relief to not only see that my fiancé is still here but also that it's still early in the morning. I'm not late for work yet, which is a bonus. I also still have plenty of time to call in sick because there is no way I can be in that office when my hangover does eventually kick in.

'I'm sorry,' I say, entering the bathroom as Tom turns the tap on and spits out his toothpaste into the sink. 'I had the worst day yesterday, and you weren't in when I got home, so I started drinking and—'

'Passed out downstairs?'

I can tell that Tom isn't impressed by my antics, and I can't blame him. I'm thirty-six, yet I'm acting like a sixteen-year-old who has just discovered the potency of booze.

'I don't know what got into me. I had way too much. I don't even drink vodka anymore, but it's all we had in and—'

'Don't worry about it. You don't have to explain

yourself to me,' he says before dropping his toothbrush into the holder and walking past me out of the bathroom.

On the face of it, it sounds like he's forgiving me for not even making it up to bed last night, but I know that's not what his words really mean. Instead, he's making a point.

He's basically saying that I don't care enough about him, so why should he care about me?

'Tom, don't be like this,' I say, following him back into the bedroom. 'We need to talk. We can't carry on like this.'

'That's the first sensible thing you've said in a long time.'

'What do you mean by that?'

'I mean, how do you think I feel going on social media to see your name being dragged through the mud because of all the wild theories and fantasies you have been spouting about your ex-boyfriends' deaths? Half the town hates you for starting false rumours about Shaun's suicide, and those who don't hate you are laughing at you.'

'They're not false rumours,' I say, but Tom doesn't want to hear it.

'But they're not the only ones who are sick of hearing these things,' he says, shaking his head. 'I'm sick of hearing them too, and I've had enough now.'

'What do you mean by that?'

Tom takes a deep breath before he answers me, and I'm not sure if it's a good thing that he paused or if I'd have been better off hearing it right away and getting it over with.

'I can't do this anymore,' he says calmly.

'Do what? What am I making you do?'

'Oh, I don't know? How about having to hear you

not only talking about your ex-boyfriends but going to their funerals or messaging them? And do you think it was nice for me to come home and find you passed out on the carpet like some wasted teenager at a house party? Is that the woman I'm marrying?'

'No, of course not!'

'It seems like it. Do you even want this wedding to go ahead?'

'Don't be stupid. Of course I do!'

'It feels like you're doing everything you can to put me off.'

'Tom, just calm down and let me speak.'

'I can't. I've got to go to work. And so have you.'

Tom looks at me in disgust before storming out of the bedroom, and I try to follow, but he slams the door behind himself, and it's enough to make me pause. I'm seething, but I'm also shocked because he has never raised his voice like that at me.

Was he serious about what he said about the wedding? Does he really think that I'm trying to put him off?

I slump down onto the edge of the bed and try to plot my next move. I know going after him while we're fired up will be a disaster, so I'll stay up here until he has left the house. I do need to shower because he's right about me not smelling my best. But first, I need to call in sick at work and not just because of how I feel. I need to spend today getting myself together, and I need to make sure I'm ready for when Tom gets back tonight so we can sort this out before it gets any worse.

I take my phone from my pocket to make the call to my office but then remember that the battery is dead, so it's useless without any charge.

Getting off the bed and dropping to my knees by the wall, I pick up the wire for the charger that is plugged into the wall and stick it into my phone, waiting impatiently for it to get enough power into it so that I can turn it on.

A couple of minutes later, I'm in, though the sound of Tom banging the kitchen cupboards downstairs reminds me that I shouldn't feel too positive about things right now. As my phone loads up, I'm just about to find the number for my office when I see the text message come through from Doris, one of the women I work with. At first, I panic because I fear that it's going to be something about how I have to come in today for an important meeting, and that's the last thing I need when I am just about to call in sick. But then I open the message and see that it's not that.

It's something much worse.

*Hi. Have you seen the news about Ash? Hope you're okay.*

I don't know what news my colleague is referring to, but I almost feel like I do. The sinking feeling in my stomach tells me that something has happened to him, just like something happened to Shaun, Calum, and Ryan.

Doris knows that Ash and I used to be together, so I expect that is the reason for her message of concern, but then again, the news of any old colleague of ours dying would be sad, so she probably would have messaged me anyway to talk about it. But I need to know exactly what has happened.

I start typing out a text asking her what the news is when I decide to just call her instead because I can't risk her not replying and leaving me sitting here paranoid.

As the phone rings, I grip the device tightly and pray that the news isn't going to be as bad as I fear. I have to believe that Ash isn't dead too. After all, I only spoke to him last night. Surely nothing bad could have happened to him since then?

'Hi, love. Are you okay?'

Doris' voice is as warm and friendly as it always is, but I have no time for returning the pleasantries.

'What's happened?' I ask her, cutting to the chase.

'Oh, love. I wasn't sure if you had heard. That's why I texted you so you could find out before you came in this morning. It's Ash. He was attacked last night.'

'Attacked? What do you mean attacked?'

'He must have been out in town. They found him lying in the street. Somebody had beaten him up.'

'Oh, my god. Is he okay?'

Doris goes uncharacteristically quiet, which gives me my answer, but I force her to put it into words anyway.

'Doris? Is he okay?'

'I'm sorry, love. He died. It's on the news. The police are looking for the person who might have done it, but—'

I've stopped listening to my colleague now because my phone has fallen from my hand, and I'm scrambling to my feet. Pulling open the bedroom door, I run for the staircase, calling out to Tom as I go.

At first, I fear that he has already left, but then I hear the sound of his car starting outside, so I jump down the last few stairs and dive for the front door, opening it as quickly as I can and running out onto the driveway.

I see him sitting behind the wheel of his car, and he's just about to reverse when he sees me racing towards him, presumably looking like a madwoman.

He goes to put his window down, but I don't even give him the chance, grabbing the door handle and pulling it open before reaching for his arm and trying to pull him out of the car.

'What the hell are you doing?' he asks me, and for a

second, he looks afraid of me. But if he's worried now, then he's got no chance when I tell him what I have to say.

'Ash is dead!' I cry, holding onto him tightly as if letting him out of my sight now will mean I'll never see him again. 'He was attacked and killed last night! That's four of my exes who have died now!'

'What? Slow down!'

'Now do you believe me?' I ask him, although it comes out sounding more like I'm begging. 'Do you?'

I don't know whether Tom actually believes me or whether he is just trying to calm me down, but he tells me that he does, and that's all it takes for me to slump down onto the driveway and cry, all the emotion of the last few weeks pouring out of me now that I'm no longer alone in this hell.

But I make sure to keep one hand on my fiancé as he sits in the driver's seat. I daren't let him out of my sight anymore.

With Ash dead, that only leaves one more ex.

And then it's Tom.

## 24

I'm back at the police station, but this time I'm not alone. Tom is with me too, and I'm glad of that because having him here means he can take over and talk for me if I get too emotional with the police officers I'm speaking to. I don't want that to be the case, but I guess it just depends on if they pay attention and take me seriously this time, doesn't it?

I asked for PC Brown when we walked in here, simply because at least with him, I wouldn't have to start at the beginning again when I ran through my sorry list of ex-boyfriends and their fates. But I was told I might have to make do with somebody else, and that's fine because I'm determined to say everything that I came here to say, and it doesn't matter who has to hear it. Fortunately, PC Brown walks through the double doors into the waiting room, and I give Tom a nudge before we stand up and make our way over to him.

I notice that the policeman looks weary when he sees me, and I'm not sure if he's not thrilled that I'm back again or whether he's just coming to the end of a night shift. But I'm about to wake him up, no doubt about that.

As PC Brown leads Tom and me into the same room that I sat in the last time I was here, I waste no time in getting to the point.

'There's been another death,' I say before the poor policeman has even had a chance to take his seat. 'Ash Sweeney. You've heard about him, right? Found beaten to death in an alleyway last night? That makes four of my exes who have died now, and try to tell me that one wasn't murder.'

I'm not prepared to apologise for how forceful I'm being, even though I can tell it is making Tom uncomfortable. He shifts awkwardly in his seat beside me, and I know he is probably wondering where I've got the confidence to talk to a police officer like this from, but he hasn't seen anything yet.

'Yes, I am aware of Mr Sweeney's death,' PC Brown says, finally settling into his seat after listening to my opening gambit. 'But like you said, it occurred late last night, so you're going to need to give us more time before we can determine exactly what happened and who might have caused it.'

'What's there to determine? The news reports said he was found face down on the street, covered in blood and bruises. I don't think he did that to himself.'

'Adele,' Tom says, putting his hand on my arm, but I brush it off.

'I came in here two days ago and told you that something was wrong. Did you even look into it? Did you investigate all the deaths I told you to look into?'

I see a flicker of frustration flash across PC Brown's face, but he's a professional and does well to quickly cover it up before giving me a professional response.

'We did look into Shaun Gibson's death again,' he

says, resting his hands in his lap as he speaks. 'And we found nothing that leads us to believe that it was anything other than suicide, as we did the first time.'

I shake my head. 'Four deaths now, one of them definitely murder and an ominous text message that lets me know that whoever is doing this is not going to stop. And that's the best you've got?'

'Adele, I think you should calm down.'

Tom's input is not welcome at this point, and I'm starting to think that him being here might not be as helpful as I had hoped it would be. At first, I was thrilled that he finally believed me, and as he drove me to the police station, I thought that whatever happened next, at least it would mean an end to the arguments we have been having lately. But if he carries on like this, then they're not going to stop.

They're only going to get worse.

Fortunately, PC Brown speaks again before I can give my fiancé a response.

'We're looking into Mr Sweeney's murder, and of course, it's concerning, not just for you but for all members of the public,' the polite police officer says. 'But you have to let us do our jobs, and we can only go on the evidence we have. I'm sorry, but there still isn't enough for us to go on when it comes to making any arrests. We don't know for sure that all these deaths are connected.'

'I'm the connection!' I cry, banging my hands on the table and causing both men seated at it to flinch. 'How many times do I have to tell you that? Whoever is doing this is going after every man I have ever been in a relationship with, and because you're doing nothing, now there's only two left!'

Perhaps wisely, neither man speaks for a moment, instead giving me the chance to simmer down. As I do, I regret turning down PC Brown's offer of a drink on the way in here because my throat is dry, and it's not just because of all the alcohol I consumed last night. It's because I've just been shouting at a policeman.

'Who would be next?' PC Brown asks me, catching me by surprise because it sounds like he is changing tack and at least humouring me now.

'Jesse Addams' I reply, my voice much lower now but my heart rate feeling just as high as it was a moment ago. 'He was my last boyfriend before I met Tom.'

'Are you still in contact with Mr Addams?'

'No.'

I make sure to answer firmly with a shake of the head, but it's not just for the benefit of the man who asked me the question. It's for Tom too because I know he will be happy to know that this is one ex I haven't been messaging lately.

'Would you be able to provide us with an address for him? Or some way of getting in touch?' PC Brown asks, taking out a notebook and pen and putting them on the table.

'I don't think so,' I reply, realising that now the policeman seems to be helping me, I suddenly am no longer able to help him.

'You don't have him on social media?' Tom asks me, but I shake my head.

'Do you know his date of birth?' PC Brown tries. 'Or any previous address?'

I do my best to recall Jesse's birthday, but I can't. We were only together for a year, but it wasn't the kind of relationship where I had time to worry about what I was going to buy him for special anniversaries. I spent more time worrying about myself than him.

But maybe I can remember his old address.

'I think he used to live on Sexton Avenue,' I say,

doing my best to visualise the flat I visited several times. 'In the tower block. The grey one. You know which one I mean?'

PC Brown nods to let me know that he does. 'What number?' he asks, making notes on his pad.

'I think it was seven,' I say, though I'm not sure. 'Or maybe it was seventeen. There was definitely a seven in there.'

PC Brown writes down both those numbers though I can tell from the look on his face that he would prefer to have something more concrete to work with. But then I suddenly remember that I actually do have something useful I can give him.

'I reported him once, back in 2015,' I say, realising that they will be able to look him up in their system.

'You did?' Tom says, presumably wondering why the hell I would call the police on my boyfriend.

I'm just about to explain to him the reason why when I remember that Tom is sitting beside me, so I pause. I have never told him what happened between Jesse and me, and the real reason why we broke up. I just mentioned he was my last boyfriend and left it at that. But now I'm going to have to bring up the full truth of the past, and it's one I have done my best to forget over the years.

'Jesse was violent towards me when we dated,' I admit, lowering my eyes to the table because just recalling that terrible time is enough to make me feel weak and vulnerable again.

'What?' Tom cries, reaching out and taking my hand as if he could somehow have protected me from it even though it happened years before he met me.

'It's okay,' I tell him, giving his hand a squeeze. 'It was a long time ago. But that's why we broke up. He hit me. More than once. One night I called the police. That's the last time I ever saw him.'

'Did he go to prison?' Tom asks, seemingly taking on the role of PC Brown now with all the questions.

'Yeah. He pleaded guilty, and there was plenty of evidence, so I didn't have to go to court. But like I say, it was a long time ago. I'm fine, seriously.'

I smile at Tom to let him know that I mean it. But then PC Brown speaks, and my smile quickly fades.

'Considering his background, how likely do you think it is that Jesse might be the person doing all of this?' he asks me.

The easy thing to do would be to dismiss that idea. After all, the text message I received seemed to be counting Jesse in the list of six potential victims. But now I'm thinking back to how violent he was towards me, as well as how much he begged for me to give him another chance as the police dragged him away, and suddenly, I'm not so sure.

## 25

I was thirty when I met Jesse Addams. As if reaching that milestone in age wasn't enough to make it a memorable year, he came along and made sure I would never forget it.

As if a precursor as to how eventful my relationship with Jesse would end up being, the way we met was just as hectic. Our paths crossed on a Friday night, only a few weeks after I had celebrated turning thirty with a group of friends, including Nicola. But when I say celebrated, I mean I just drank so much that I forgot about how old I was getting and also about the fact that I was no nearer to finding a stable partner to settle down with in life.

My friends had spent the latter part of my birthday evening trying to console me with assurances that it was only a matter of time until I met Mr Right, and telling me that I just had to stay positive and open to opportunity. Despite all the tears and tequila that night, I took their advice on board, and sure enough, it wasn't long until a new man came into my life.

So how did it happen? Did he sweep me off my feet

in a crowded bar? Get introduced to me through a mutual friend? Or did he stop me on my way to work one morning to tell me that he needed to have my phone number so that he could contact me at a later date?

It turned out to be the latter, but it wasn't as romantic as it might sound.

Basically, Jesse crashed into the back of my car at a set of traffic lights.

I'd been sitting behind the wheel, making my morning commute, my eyes like slits and my head still longing for my pillow, when I felt a huge jolt and realised I'd been rear-ended. Fortunately, I wasn't hurt in the impact, so I was able to get out of my vehicle quickly enough and rush around to the back of it to assess the damage, both on the driver behind and on my own car.

Luckily, the other driver was okay, which was a lot more than could be said for my poor car, which now had a huge dent in the back end, although it was still just about driveable to get me the rest of the way to my office that morning.

As the driver responsible for the accident apologised profusely, I surprised myself by not feeling as angry or despondent as I could have done after such an incident. Maybe it was the adrenaline that came with being in a mild car crash, but as I stood there and looked at this apologetic driver, I thought about how handsome he was and about how I wished we'd met under slightly more normal circumstances.

He told me his name was Jesse, and he also told me that he accepted full responsibility for the incident, which was very kind of him, even if it was simply just the truth. Then he told me that we would have to swap insurance details, asking for my name and number so we could get out of the way of the rest of the other traffic and sort this out later. It had certainly been the most unusual way I had given another man my personal details, but after swapping digits, we went our separate ways, and I prepared to be contacted by his insurers.

What I wasn't prepared for was to be contacted by him asking me if I would like to go for a drink.

I said yes, not just because I had found him attractive at the scene of the incident but also because I could tell he was feeling guilty about causing it, and I hadn't wanted to make him feel any worse. Our first date took place three nights later and went really well, helped no doubt by the fact that we had already broken the ice about as dramatically as any first-daters could do with the minor car crash a few days earlier. That meant we could skip all the awkward getting-to-know-you parts and instead engage in some light-hearted banter straight away, with me teasing him about his driving skills and him joking that he had simply been distracted by catching a glimpse of my beauty in my rear-view mirror.

Perhaps it was because I was in my thirties then, or maybe it was because how we met expedited things somewhat, but it didn't take us long to get serious, and Jesse became a regular visitor to my one-bedroom flat just outside the town centre. I had bought the small property after deciding that I couldn't rent forever while waiting for a man to settle down with, but then Jesse came along and made me start to think that I'd been a bit hasty. He had his own place too, although I only stayed there rarely because it wasn't anywhere near as nice as mine, so it meant we potentially had two properties to sell if we were going to make the big step of moving in together.

But those plans came crashing down almost as

dramatically as when our two cars had collided on the day we met just a few months later on a stormy night in Blackburn.

I know I like to overdo it every now and again when it comes to alcohol, but Jesse was on a different level to me. I first noticed that he seemed to have an unhealthy relationship with booze during some of our early dates, where I suspected he had already been drinking a little before he turned up. At the time, I put it down to him just being nervous, and I thought it was endearing until I got to know him better and realised that he wasn't shy; he was an alcoholic.

It took me a while to feel like we were close enough for me to be comfortable broaching the subject with him, but it happened one Saturday night after we had been out in town together. We had made it back to my flat, soaking wet from the heavy rain outside, and I'd presumed we would just go to bed considering how late it was and how drunk we both were. But Jesse had other ideas, and instead of following me into the bedroom, he proceeded to raid my cupboards for more alcohol, ultimately settling for a bottle of wine I didn't even remember having.

Seeing him sitting up drinking wine for no good reason other than the fact that he needed more booze in his bloodstream was the moment when I decided to broach the subject of his alcohol intake with him. But that was a mistake. Jesse turned quickly, showing me a side of him that I had never seen before. But by then, it was too late.

I was already on the floor, desperately trying to protect myself as he rained heavy blows down on me.

Jesse must have punched me over twenty times that night, to the face and body, before he stopped and crawled off me, going back to his wine while I cowered on the carpet and just felt grateful that it had ended before he had killed me. It had taken me a while to pluck up the courage to ask him to leave, which he eventually did, though he took the bottle of wine with him, and I spent the whole of the next day hiding in my bedroom, afraid to come out and face the world. But I had no choice but to the day after that because I had to be at work for an important meeting, so I did my best to cover my bruises with make-up and went into the office. I hadn't done a good enough job, however, and it hadn't taken long for somebody to notice my injuries, and after an emotional discussion with HR, I decided that I not only had to end things with Jesse but inform the police about what he had done to me.

That was six years ago, and I have only seen Jesse once since that horrible night. He surprised me three years ago by turning up at my office, telling me that he had recently been released from prison and that he wanted to apologise for what he had done to me. I could tell that he was sober, as well as the fact that he meant what he was saying, but that hadn't stopped me feeling afraid, which was why I turned down his offer of going for a coffee and instead got myself away from him as quickly as I could. Fortunately, he had left me alone after that, so I hadn't had to contact the police and give them his name again.

Until today.

Now I have just given his name to PC Brown, and while I initially did so because I suspected he might be the next victim, now I'm thinking that he could very well be the person behind everything that has been happening to me and my exes lately. He was obviously still hoping to rekindle a romance with me after he got released a few years ago, which I had quickly denied him, so there is the chance he has been feeling angry about that. Then there's also his history of violence, which not only makes him somebody capable of doing nasty things to other people but could make him a prime suspect for the vicious beating and subsequent murder of my ex before him, Ash.

PC Brown has promised me that he will track down Jesse and question him about his movements recently to see if there are any parts of his story that cause concern. But even if not, and it turns out that Jesse is innocent of this, then he will be suitably warned about the fact that he is likely to be coming to harm in the near future.

It feels weird to think of my violent ex as being a potential victim after what he did to me, but there is no doubt now that with Ash gone, if Jesse is not the man behind it, then he will be the one to be targeted next.

But it's out of my hands now and is a matter for the police, just like it was on the day when I made that phone call and told them that I had been physically abused by my boyfriend.

The police did a good job of sorting that problem out for me.

I can only hope they do an even better job of sorting this one out now.

## 26

There has been a big change in Tom ever since he found out about my abusive ex. No longer is he doubting me and my paranoid thoughts, but he is also being way more caring and attentive than he ever was, even during the best times of our relationship. It's obvious that he was shocked to learn about what Jesse did to me, and not just because I had kept it a secret from him. He was shocked because I imagine it kills him inside to know that I had to suffer so much at that time at the hands of another man.

It's been two days since we visited the police station together, and in that time, Tom has made sure to let me know that he is there for me if I need to talk about anything. Of course, as my fiancé, I always knew he was there anyway, but maybe the fact that I had kept some things about my past from him has made him feel like he wasn't doing a good enough job of that. But I have made it clear that there are no more skeletons in my closet now. There are no more secrets to be shared and, hopefully, no more reasons for us to ever argue again. The social media storm is dying down now, Nicola is adamant that it wasn't her who leaked the information, and all we can do now is try to get on with our lives while the police look into Jesse, either to find out if he is guilty of anything or to at least warn him that he might be in danger. That means we are going full steam ahead with our wedding planning after a few days of losing our way with it, which is why we are back at Heron's Barn again to sign the necessary paperwork to say that we will hold the ceremony at this venue.

As expected, Rachel, our soon-to-be wedding planner, is all smiles when she sees the two of us waiting for her in the reception area.

'Adele! Tom! How lovely to see you again!'

She gives each of us a warm hug before leading us away from the reception, but instead of taking us back into the meeting room where we sat on our earlier visit, she takes us out through the entrance to the barn and into the bright sunlight of what is a beautiful day in this part of the world.

'I thought we should make the most of the weather and hold the meeting out here, if that's okay with you guys?' she suggests as she leads us across the patio area towards a white table and chair set that is positioned to overlook the immaculate grounds of this pretty place.

'That's fine,' I tell her, and a quick check on Tom's expression lets me know that he has no objections too, not that I thought he would do. It really is a beautiful day here, and it's nice to be able to get to sit outside and take in the picturesque gardens around us, gardens that we will eventually be standing in on our wedding day as a photographer runs around us and tries to get the perfect shots.

'Lovely, well, take a seat, and we'll get started,' Rachel says as she sits down on one of the white chairs and starts to rummage through the stack of papers on the table, all of which have been protected from the wind by a heavy paperweight bearing this venue's logo.

We're only a few minutes into running through the practicalities of having a wedding on our desired date next summer when we're interrupted very politely by a young man in a smart uniform, holding a tray with three glasses of lemonade on it.

As the three of us accept our drinks and clink glasses beneath a clear blue sky, it's easy to think that all is well in life and that these next twelve months are going to be filled with nothing but exciting times as we settle on the details for the big day, as well as enjoy the less stressful aspects of getting married like the stag and hen dos. But as life so often has a habit of doing, it's not long until I get a reminder that not everything is perfect. In fact, it's far from it.

I ignore the buzzing of my mobile phone on the table in front of me at first as I try to be polite and remain focused on what Rachel was telling me about food options for the wedding breakfast. But I had to look at it when it rang again, and that's when I saw that PC Brown was calling me.

'I'm so sorry. I have to take this,' I say, picking up my phone and getting up from my seat.

'That's okay. We can wait,' Rachel tells me with a smile, and I hear her ask Tom about his day job as I rush away from the table to somewhere more private so I can take the call.

I choose the shady area around the side of the building as a good enough spot to answer.

'Hello?'

'Hi, Adele. It's PC Brown here. I hope I'm not inter-rupting anything?'

'No, not at all. What is it?'

I know that receiving a phone call from a police

officer would generally not be considered a good thing, so I'd rather just cut to the chase and find out what it's about.

'I was able to find Jesse on our system, and I visited him at his home this morning,' PC Brown says as I feel my body temperature cooling now that I'm out of the glare of the hot sun.

'And?'

'I asked him to account for his whereabouts on the evening of Ash's death, and he was able to provide an alibi, which I have since been able to corroborate. Jesse is definitely not responsible for Ash's murder.'

'Did you ask him about the other deaths?'

'No, solely based on the fact that those are still being treated as non-suspicious.'

'Did you warn him, then?'

'I told Jesse to be vigilant for the foreseeable future. Avoid being out late at night or alone if he can help it, although of course, he wanted to know why.'

'What did you tell him?'

'I didn't want to mention your name, so I told him that we were just taking precautions while we investigated Ash's murder.'

'Thank you,' I say, pleased that the policeman didn't let Jesse know that the visit had anything to do with me. But maybe that's not such a good thing because it might be better if Jesse knows the full story of what's going on. That way, he will know how seriously to take this.

'So what happens next?' I ask, hoping that this isn't all PC Brown is going to do for me. Just because Jesse is innocent in this case, it doesn't mean that there isn't still another dangerous person out there who needs to be stopped.

'I'll do some more digging into Calum's and Ryan's deaths. The final report into the cause of the car crash should be available soon, as well as the clarification from the fire service down in Portsmouth.'

'Just do what you can. Please,' I urge the policeman, who promises me that he will before we say goodbye, and he hangs up.

I take a few seconds to process the conversation I just had before I walk back around the corner of this building and back into the bright sunlight, where I will rejoin my fiancé and our wedding planner as we continue to discuss options for what is going to be an expensive day.

When I feel like I'm ready, I head back to the table with my phone in my hand, noticing as I go that the conversation at the table seems to have dried up between Tom and Rachel. I guess it was always going to be weird between me and her, seeing how she used to be my best friend, but I would have thought that there wouldn't have been any reason for awkwardness between her and my fiancé. But it seems that way because both Tom and Rachel are leaning back in their chairs and texting on their phones. I guess they are waiting for me to come back so they can just get on with things again.

With that in mind, I hurry on my way, but before I can reach the table, I feel my phone vibrate in my hand. Looking down at the screen, it's initially tricky to read the message that I have just received because of the bright sunlight, but I turn my back to it, and then I'm able to get a better look.

That's when I see that it is another message from the mystery person who contacted me earlier.

*One to go. And then it's Tom's turn.*

I feel physically sick as I read the words on the

screen, and the hot weather is doing nothing to help ease the wave of nausea passing over me.

My first instinct is to call PC Brown straight back and give him the news, but then I decide to try my luck again with calling the number to see if anybody answers this time.

Holding the phone to my ear, I wait for the ring tone to start. But all I get is the message that the number I am calling is unavailable. Whoever sent the message must have turned their phone off immediately after they sent it.

I feel the beads of sweat building on my forehead as I turn back to the table and prepare to bring this meeting to a close so I can get Tom and we can head back to the police station. But then I notice that Rachel is no longer using her mobile phone. She was texting on it only a moment ago, but now it's just sitting on the table in front of her.

I wonder…

Without warning, I rush towards the table and pick up her mobile phone, tapping the screen to check if it is turned on.

'Hey!' Rachel cries, obviously wondering what the hell I'm doing, as does Tom, who drops his phone quickly and looks up at me as if I'm mad.

But I'm not. Rachel's phone is turned off.

Is she the one who has been texting me?

'What are you doing?' Rachel asks as I hold down the button on the side of her phone to turn it back on. I want to check her messages and see if it really is her. But before I get the chance to, she swipes the phone from my hand.

'Adele, what are you doing?' she asks me again.

'It's you, isn't it? You're the one who's been doing all this?'

'What the hell are you talking about?'

She might pretend like she's all grown up and doing a good job as a professional wedding planner, but the look on her face right now is the same one that she wore when we had our first big argument back in school, not long before our days as best friends officially came to an end. She looks annoyed, slightly spiteful and most of all like she knows she has done something wrong.

'My exes. What did you do to them all?' I ask her as Tom gets up from his seat, clearly aware that he is about to have a potential catfight on his hands.

'Adele, you're not making any sense,' Rachel replies before looking at Tom as if to say that I'm the crazy woman here and she is the innocent one. But the way she is looking at him is too much for me, and I can't help myself.

I go for her, determined to get her mobile phone back and check her messages before she has the chance to worm her way out of this one.

Grabbing her arm, I pull her towards me, hoping the phone will fall from her grasp. The sudden forward motion of her body bumps her into the table, and the glasses of lemonade topple over, soaking the wedding brochures before the glasses roll off and smash on the concrete patio beneath us. But I don't care about that as I continue to try to wrestle the phone from her hand, and even the feeling of Tom trying to pull me off isn't enough to slow me down.

Before I know it, the table has toppled over too, and I'm guessing Rachel and I are only seconds away from joining it on the floor until the waiter who served us the drinks comes to Tom's aid and helps drag me off the wedding planner before we can cause any more damage.

'Get her out of here!' Rachel cries to the poor waiter

as she storms away in the direction of the barn, but my attempts to go after her are halted by Tom, who refuses to let me pass him.

'It's her!' I tell him, tears in my eyes as I watch her walk away. 'She's the one who's been doing it all!'

But Tom says nothing, instead telling the waiter that we are going, and as he leads me away back towards the car park, I feel furious that he isn't as desperate to get to Rachel as I am.

I feel even worse when I turn around and see her watching me leave through the window of the barn.

## 27

'You're joking,' Nicola says just after I have finished telling her all about the dramatic events at the wedding venue yesterday.

The sheepish look on my face must tell her that I am not, and the reason I'm looking that way is because despite what I believed when I tried to take Rachel's phone from her, I turned out to be wrong. My former best friend is not the person behind the mysterious texts that I have been receiving, and not the person who has been targeting my ex-boyfriends.

I know that now because Tom and I went straight from Heron's Barn to the police station yesterday, where I demanded to see PC Brown before showing him the second message I received and refusing to leave until he assured me that he would investigate Rachel further. But I didn't know that at the time. If I had, it would have saved me a whole lot of embarrassment later.

Rachel was a lot more willing to give up her phone to an investigating officer than she was to me, and they were able to determine that she was not the one sending the messages. PC Brown gave me that news at midday today, although it came after I had already had a good idea that I had been wrong in my assumption.

Needless to say, Tom and I will not be getting married at Heron's Barn next year. I think my behaviour was enough to curtail those plans yesterday, although the email I received from the owner of the venue this morning made it official. The message was polite but firm, telling me that based on 'an incident' at the property, we should consider any agreement terminated and that Heron's Barn wished us all the best with our future nuptials, as long as they didn't take place on their premises.

In normal times, the fact that I had just lost my wedding venue might have sent me into a blind panic, but these are anything but normal times. The fact that the second message told me that Tom was next is enough to stop me worrying about the wedding and, instead, spend all my time anxiously praying that the police catch this person before they get to my fiancé.

PC Brown has promised to speed up the investigation into Calum's death, as well as try again with the police in Portsmouth to learn more about Ryan's. But I fear it isn't going to be enough. Both Jesse and Tom are still out there unprotected, and the killer could strike at any moment.

I begged Tom not to go to work today, insisting that he stay home with me until we knew for sure that he was safe. But he told me that he had an important presentation to give and that he couldn't miss it despite the fact that it would be wiser for him to lie low until the police have a chance to arrest a suspect.

That's the problem, though.

There are no suspects now.

The guy at the gym. My violent ex. The woman I used to be best friends with. I suspected them all at one time or another, but where has that got me? I'm still no nearer to knowing who might be the one coming after every man I have ever been intimate with.

As I usually do in times of struggle, I called Nicola and told her that I needed a drink with her. I had come to the thinking that it hadn't been her who had leaked my worries about Shaun's suicide because she was my best friend and I could trust her. I felt bad for ignoring her recently and asked if she could forgive me, which she could. Then I asked her about meeting up, but there was one condition. She had to come to me. I'm not leaving the house today, preferring privacy over going out and potentially doing something else that might make my situation worse. The police have told me to contact them immediately if I receive another message, and I certainly will, but other than that, I'm lying low, which means no work, no gym, no nothing.

'This is really bad,' Nicola says after watching me take another gulp of my drink. 'I can't believe the police have no idea who this might be.'

'No idea at all,' I confirm, shaking my head. 'At least they know for sure that Ash was murdered, which means they're taking that death seriously.'

'I wonder why the killer would do that.'

'What do you mean?'

'Well, all your other exes' deaths were made to look like accidents or at least not suspicious. But why change it up for Ash? It's almost as if they want the police to be looking for them now.'

'Maybe they do,' I say, shrugging my shoulders. 'It's like the messages. They are obviously teasing me and want me to try to stop them before they get to Tom. But

I have no idea how to if I can't figure out who it might be.'

I can see that Nicola is desperate to help me, but just like everybody else I've told my sorry story to, she doesn't seem to have much to offer. But then she suddenly sits forward and puts her glass of wine down, as if struck by a sudden thought.

'Wait, remember when we said it had to be somebody who you knew because otherwise, how would they have known about all your exes?'

'Yeah…'

'Well, what's the one place where somebody could see who you were in a relationship with at any time?'

I think for a second before realising what she is getting at.

'Social media,' I say.

'Exactly. So whoever is doing this must be one of your friends online. That's how they know who to go after and in what order.'

Oh, my god, I think she is right.

Putting my own glass of wine down beside hers on the coffee table, I pick up my phone and open one of the apps before quickly scrolling to the part that lists all my friends and followers.

The problem is that there are over six hundred of them.

'Wow, you have a lot more than me,' Nicola says as she watches me scrolling through the sea of names and faces that I am connected to online, although I know that's not because she is in any way unpopular. It's simply because, unlike me, she didn't go to university or spend three years travelling, meaning her social circle stayed fairly small while mine was growing by the day at one point.

'How the hell do I narrow it down?' I ask as my

thumb moves across the screen, and I see several names move past, none of whom give me any reason to think that they might be the ones behind this.

'I don't know, but maybe it's not your job to,' Nicola says. 'Give that list to the police and let them figure it out for you.'

'You really think that would work? They haven't done much so far with two names. What chance have they got with six hundred?'

'You have to try something, don't you?' Nicola reminds me, and she is right. The only certainty now is that if I do nothing, Jesse will die next.

And then, just like the ominous second message says, it's Tom's turn.

'You really think it's one of these people?' I ask, still scrolling through all the profile photos of the people who have been a part of my life at one time or another.

'I think it's our best bet at the moment,' Nicola tells me, and she isn't wrong there.

The longer I spend scrolling, the more I feel uncomfortable about the thought that somebody has been monitoring my activity online for years, keeping tabs and taking notes. Of course, I always knew that sharing photos and thoughts with my friends and followers on social media was hardly the best thing to do if I wanted privacy, but there's a big difference between sharing things because you think your acquaintances will like them and giving somebody everything they need to form a deadly plot against you.

Social media gets a lot of bad press for having a dark side, but if Nicola turns out to be right and the killer is one of the people on here, then this has to be a contender for one of the worst things to ever come from it. But she must be right. How else could somebody have known about Shaun, Calum, Ryan, Ash, and Jesse and the order in which I dated them?

I wish I could just delete my social media accounts now, but I can't.

They're the only way I have of narrowing this down before it's too late.

## 28

I 'm still online, tormenting myself by looking at all the people who have seen every single one of my status updates over the years, when Tom gets back from work. He's later than usual, though I suspect that is because he had the presentation to get through.

'How did it go?' I ask him as I hear him dropping his briefcase in the hallway and tossing his car keys onto the bottom step of the staircase, where he always keeps them.

'Fine,' he replies before I hear his footsteps going up the stairs. 'I'm just going to jump in the shower.'

He doesn't usually do anything when he gets in before giving me a kiss and asking about my day, but I guess today is different. Maybe the presentation didn't go well. I really hope that's not it, mainly because if it was a disaster, it was probably because all the drama and stress of these last few weeks has gotten on top of him and knocked him off his game. I guess it's tough to present when you're worried about somebody out there who might be planning to kill you.

Feeling terrible about how much stress all of this

must be putting on my fiancé, I leave my phone on the sofa and head for the stairs myself, determined to spend the next part of the evening doing everything I can to cheer Tom up and keep him positive. But my intentions aren't purely selfless. They're also because I know that if Tom starts to crumble, then I've got no chance of keeping it together.

I can already hear the shower running as I reach the top of the stairs, and I wonder if I'm going to catch him just in time before he gets under the water. But maybe it wouldn't be a bad thing if he's already in there. I could just slip my clothes off quietly and join him.

I doubt he would mind that.

But then I open the bedroom door and see that he hasn't made it into the shower yet, although he is almost fully undressed, barring his boxer shorts and socks, which he is in the process of taking off too. That's how I am able to see not only his naked torso but also all the cuts and bruises that are covering it.

'Oh, my god, what happened?' I ask him as I rush into the bedroom.

It's clear from the look on Tom's face that he hadn't heard me coming up the stairs, and he has no chance to cover himself up before I reach him to get a closer look.

'It's nothing,' he says as I reach out for one of his arms, which I can see has a dark bruise on it as well as a couple of scratches.

'It doesn't look like nothing! Where did you get these?' I ask him, showering him with questions before he can wash away his wounds. I'm not sure how fresh they are. Maybe he got them today. Maybe they are a couple of days old. The only way I'll know is if Tom tells me the truth.

But it seems like he's not willing to do that.

'I'm fine. Just leave it,' he says, pulling his arm away from me and heading for the bathroom.

'It's obviously not fine!' I cry, following him into the en-suite, where the heat from the hot shower has caused the mirror to steam up. 'Why won't you tell me what happened?'

'Just leave it, Adele,' he tries again, and it's clear he wants to close the bathroom door on me, but I don't let him, standing in the way and staring at him until he gives me answers.

'Tell me!' I demand, and I realise this is a crucial point in our relationship. Either he does as I ask, and we can salvage this, or he refuses to, and things can only get worse for us from here. Fortunately, after a tense moment, he chooses the sensible option.

'I got into a bit of a fight at work,' he admits, shaking his head as if to reinforce how ridiculous it sounds.

'You did what?'

'It was stupid. But I'm fine, seriously.'

'You don't look fine.'

'I am. It was just a little scuffle. Nothing major.'

'Who was it with?'

He pauses for a second before answering, though I'm not sure why he would do so. It's not as if I know any people at his work that would make him want to keep it private.

'Allan in accounts,' he says eventually.

'You had a fight with someone in accounts?' I ask sceptically.

'Yeah, it's ridiculous, I know. We had a disagreement over some of the numbers for the presentation. Remember? The one I told you about? Anyway, things got heated, and we ended up being pulled off each other.'

'You got pulled off each other? By whom?'

'Some of the other guys in the office.'

'So what happens now? What did HR say?'

'My manager has sorted it all out. There's nothing to worry about.'

'It doesn't sound like there's nothing to worry about. My fiancé just started a fight with somebody in his office, and he looks like he got beaten up!'

'I'm fine, seriously. It looks worse than it feels.'

I stare at him, but it's not the dark bruises that worry me now so much as the look on his face. He would be forgiven for looking embarrassed or guilty, or even just plain stupid, but he doesn't look any of those things.

Instead, he just looks like he is lying.

I stand in front of him for a few moments, hoping that he is going to speak again and acknowledge that he hasn't been truthful with me before putting things right immediately. But he doesn't do that, simply opting to say no more and presumably hoping that I'll leave it at that and walk away.

In the end, I don't know what else to do, so I turn and leave the bathroom, and the sound of the en-suite door locking behind me confirms that Tom couldn't wait for me to leave.

As I stand there in the bedroom, listening to him under the water in the shower, I feel like I'm at a cross-roads. All this time, I have been trying to figure out who the mystery person could be in my life who has been tormenting me and targeting my exes.

But what if that person was right under my nose and I just couldn't see it.

What if it's Tom?

The thought is a crazy one, but the more I think about it, the more I worry that it makes sense. He knows the name of all my exes, even though he pretended not to the other day. He gets agitated whenever I bring them up, and even though I always thought it wasn't jealousy, maybe it was. And now there's the fact that he is covered in cuts and bruises just a few days after Ash was found beaten to death in town.

Is that how Tom ended up with those injuries? Did Ash fight back before he died?

I feel as if all the oxygen has been sucked out of the house, so I rush to the bedroom window and open it, leaning my head out and taking a deep breath before I put myself at further risk of being sick. The fresh air helps me, and I can feel myself calming down, although it's only a temporary thing. As soon as I lean back into the bedroom, I can hear the sound of my fiancé in the shower again, and it's the sound that tells me that I'm now living with a man whom I no longer trust.

He never lies to me. Not about anything. That's how I could tell that he was lying to me then.

But why? What is he hiding?

And how the hell do I find out?

## 29

Unlike with all the previous suspects I have 'identified' over these last few weeks, I am being much more cautious in revealing my beliefs this time. Acting impulsively has led to embarrassment and false panic in the past, so now, I am going to take my time and attempt to gather some real evidence so that I don't put two and two together and come up with five again. But there's another reason for my caution, and it's not just down to a fear of making a fool of myself or wasting any more police time.

It's because the suspect I have in mind now is my fiancé.

Tom came downstairs after his shower and made a point of getting me to sit down and listen to him while he explained how he got the cuts and bruises on his body. At first, I was hoping he was going to tell me the truth, leaving behind his stupid story about a workplace scuffle, and actually give me an idea of what is really going on. But no such luck. He stuck to his story. He said he had a fight at work.

He is still lying to me.

I asked him if he had been suspended or disciplined or even fired if that was the case. After all, employees can hardly go around fighting with colleagues and not expect some form of punishment. But Tom told me that other than a meeting with HR, there was to be no action taken going forward, which I found very hard to believe. But what am I supposed to do? Isn't it my job to trust the man I love? If I don't believe him, then who would?

So why am I finding it so difficult?

That conversation took place an hour ago before Tom told me that he was having an early night. He asked if I wanted to join him, but I told him that I had a few things to do before bed, which was a lie of my own, but nowhere, I thought, near on the scale of his recent one. In truth, I just felt like I needed some space from him and I seriously doubt I'll be able to fall asleep easily beside a man whom I no longer feel like I can trust. That's why he's upstairs now, and I'm down here at the kitchen table, mulling things over and trying to decide what to do next.

The police station would be my first port of call if I had a new suspect. I'd walk in and ask to see PC Brown before telling him everything I had and urging him to investigate. But I haven't done that this time, mainly because I'm terrified of what the police officer might discover if he does look into Tom.

Running through the criteria that Nicola helped me establish to track down the person who has been killing my exes and sending me creepy messages, I realise that Tom ticks every box. He knows about my relationship history, not only from social media, but because I told him about it when we started dating. He obviously has my phone number, so it would be easy for him to send me those messages from a second device. I felt another wave of nausea pass over me ten minutes ago when I remembered that he too had been texting on a mobile phone just like Rachel when I wrongly accused her of sending the messages during that ill-fated wedding meeting. And then there's the third thing, which is most likely going to be of greatest interest to PC Brown if I was to voice my suspicions to him about my fiancé.

It's that Tom could be considered to have a motive to do something like this.

He could be seen as the jealous partner, envious of my former lovers and bitter enough to want to do something about it.

All those times I used to think that it was sweet for Tom to not want to hear me talk too much about my past relationships.

Those times don't seem so innocent anymore.

But then there's the other part of me that tells me that I am wrong, and Tom isn't the person behind this. I guess that would be my heart trying to overrule my head, but I have to listen to both sides and consider everything. This is the man I am engaged to, the man I was willing to give up everything else for just to be with, so I would think I would have a pretty good idea of the person he really is. Is he capable of murder? I just can't believe it. Then again, I wouldn't have thought he was capable of getting into a fight, and the evidence on his body clearly proves that he has done just that.

But what if it was just a fight? What if somebody in his office had made a comment after noticing that social media hasn't exactly been kind to me over these last few days since I sparked the rumours about Shaun's suicide being something else? Maybe Tom was just defending my honour and sticking up for me? I have to think that is more likely than him going around killing people.

But then why wouldn't he just tell me so? Unless he's just trying to protect me.

What if all he has ever done is try to protect me?

I stand up from the kitchen table and go towards the door, suddenly feeling like I've been a terrible partner for having all these crazy thoughts and not being on Tom's side. Here I am downstairs, mulling over whether or not he could be a murderer, when he is lying in bed upstairs on his own, probably wishing he'd just got engaged to somebody who appreciated him more and didn't have such an eventful past. Not only have I had more than my fair share of ex-lovers, but some of them have been cheaters and abusers, so Tom could be forgiven for wondering what the hell he has got himself into. And now he has to put up with the fact that those exes are turning up dead, which has everything to do with me and nothing to do with him. He's just an unlucky bystander, caught up in my past when all he ever wanted was to get married to me and live a quiet life.

I'm going to go and get into bed with him and tell him that I'm sorry for doubting him. I'm going to tell him that I love him and am extremely grateful for all the support he has given me over these last few weeks ever since my life has been turned upside down. And then I am going to promise that whatever happens going forward, we will stick together and make sure that we come out of this stronger than ever, even while the potential threat to his life is still hanging over our heads.

That sounds like a good plan to me, and it certainly makes me feel better than the other one I was considering, which involved another visit to the police station and a conversation with PC Brown.

But like all my other plans in life, it doesn't take long for them to fall apart spectacularly.

The loud knock on the front door as I am walking past it on my way to the stairs makes me jump, not just because it was unexpected. It's after ten o'clock.

Who the hell would be banging on our door at this time?

The frosted glass covering half of the door gives little away other than a dark figure standing on the other side, so I have no choice but to open it if I want to find out who it is. But the second I do, I really wish I hadn't.

That was the moment when everything changed.

First of all, I realised that the dark figure on the other side of the frosted glass wasn't alone. He was with several others, and they were all wearing police uniforms. That first officer told me why they were here, but it was just a blur of words, and the only real sentence that I processed and understood was when they asked me if my fiancé was in the property.

I told them that he was before asking them why they needed to know that, but by then, it was too late. They were already making their way past me, entering my home and spreading out.

As I stood there in my hallway with the cold air from the open door rushing into my warm house, I demanded to know what was going on, but I got no answers. All the police officers seemed far too busy and focused to stop to give me those, and I remember wishing that PC Brown were here because I was sure that he would be decent enough to let me know what was happening. But I couldn't see his face amongst all the unrecognisable ones rushing through my hallway and up my stairs, so I went after them to try to get answers.

I left the officers who were downstairs and instead followed the ones who had gone upstairs, where my fiancé was, wanting to make sure he wasn't as startled as I was when the police barged in on him in a few seconds. But I wasn't quick enough, and by the time I made it to our bedroom, Tom was already awake, sitting up in his bed with a stunned expression on his face.

Then I saw the flash of the handcuffs coming out, and my poor fiancé was pulled from his bed and pushed against the wall, where his hands were dragged behind his back.

If all of that wasn't enough to send me into a panic, then the next words out of the arresting officer's mouth were.

'Tom Barton, I'm arresting you on suspicion of murder.'

## 30

It's every young girl's dream to have a big white wedding, isn't it?

The dress. The flowers. The Prince Charming waiting at the altar as you make your way down the aisle, all eyes turned in your direction, in awe of the vision of beauty passing before them. But I was different. I didn't dream about my wedding day when I was a child. I didn't play dress-up with my mum's things and pretend to be walking down the aisle, practising my pose and posture in front of the mirror. I didn't even like boys at all for the longest time, so why would I want to marry one? But like most things in life, that changed. My teenage years saw me start to notice the opposite sex more and eventually crave their attention rather than see it as a nuisance. My twenties saw me actively seek out romance, or at least act on my feelings of lust on a more regular basis – but even then, I was still too young and too excitable to seriously entertain thoughts of a wedding day. But then I reached my thirties, and that was when I suddenly decided that not only did I like the company of men, I needed it. I craved the stability as well as the companionship. I didn't want to be alone, and I didn't just want to settle for meaningless one-night stands or for men who promised me the world but couldn't deliver it.

What I wanted was a loyal and loving partner whom I could be with forever.

In other words, I wanted to get married.

But after the emotional and physical disaster that was Jesse, I was understandably wary of what I thought I wanted. After all, it had been my blind pursuit of love with him that had led to me missing or ignoring all the signs that he had a serious drinking problem, right up until the point that he was violent towards me while under the influence. If only I'd have been more cautious with him and been willing to take things slowly, then I might have been able to see the danger signs and get out before I got hurt, but I didn't. That was because I was too busy worrying about being left on the scrapheap of life, single forever and destined to never have my big day in that white dress.

Then I met Tom.

Unlike all my previous boyfriends, my first encounter with him was not in the real world, but rather, the virtual one. Yes, Tom and I met on a dating app. It's the modern way, and it's the quickest and most efficient way of finding a date, and at the age of thirty-three, I needed speed. I didn't want to waste any more precious time going on several dates with guys who just weren't right for me, only to have to start back at the beginning again, older but none the wiser as to how to conquer this silly game called love. That was why the apps were perfect, even though I initially refused to give them a go despite Nicola's assurances that they really were worth it. But in the end, I bit the bullet, downloaded a few of them, and started seeing what was out there.

Tom's photo caught my eye immediately. He looked dashing in his profile photo, wearing a suit and tie and smiling warmly into the camera. His bio was also appealing, saying he enjoyed travelling, movies, and socialising on the weekend, which is obviously code for getting drunk on a Saturday night, which was great because I loved to do all those things too. But the best thing of all was that I saw the colour at the top of his profile, which told me that he had already seen my profile and indicated his own interest. All I had to do to open the gates of communication between us was indicate my interest in return.

I did just that, and before I knew it, the man in the photo on my mobile phone screen was sitting opposite me in an Italian restaurant, sipping his red wine, eating his meatballs, and asking me more about myself. Nicola, and indeed the rest of society, was right.

Online dating was fast.

I, on the other hand, was not. After my previous relationship had ended so badly, I was determined to take my time with this new one. Much to Tom's frustration, I kept him waiting a few weeks before we shared our first kiss. It took two months before I allowed him into my home, and three before he made it into my bed. I knew that I was risking losing him by going slowly, but I was willing to take that chance to learn everything I could about him, as well as let him know everything about me. That way, there would be no surprises in the future. That was why I made sure to be honest about my past boyfriends with him, only excluding the part about when Jesse had been violent, simply because I didn't want either his sympathy or for him to think that I was some broken woman in need of a man to put her back together. I wasn't. I was simply a woman in the prime of her life, finally mature enough to handle an adult relationship, but only willing to respect somebody as far as they would respect me.

Thankfully, I didn't have to worry about that with Tom because he respected me right from the start. He was patient when I made him wait. He was kind when I needed a favour. And he was brilliant when I was looking for someone to dazzle me.

I knew when we moved in together that he was the one. Unlike my past relationships, where I always felt like either I or my partner was giving more than the other one, this time, everything was balanced and fair. I hadn't been ready for Shaun and Calum in my younger days, letting them go as soon as I realised that I couldn't give them what they wanted from me. I had been scarred after Ryan had told me that he wished to go another way after our travels together, taking a long time to realise that just because two people love each other, it doesn't mean that they want the same things from life. And I had been naïve and foolish with Ash and Jesse, allowing myself to not only be walked all over by an adulterer but physically threatened and violated by an abusive person.

But all that experience had shaped me into the woman I was when I met Tom, and it was that level of preparedness that meant that the three years we were together up until the moment he proposed were just perfect.

And suddenly, my white wedding was going to be a reality.

If life has taught me anything, it's that dreams come true.

But nightmares do too.

Ever since Tom proposed, I have been terrified of

losing him. A car crash. Cancer. A freak accident in the house where he falls down the stairs and breaks his neck. I know it wasn't healthy to think like that, but I also know it wasn't unusual. I Googled it and found forums filled with other people just like me, men and women who had been lucky enough to find their perfect partners but who now lived with that constant dread that something terrible might happen to take it all away from them.

Now I am one of the unlucky ones.

My dream relationship has fallen apart, and that perfect partner I was so afraid of losing has been lost. But it wasn't disaster, disease, or sheer bad luck that took him away from me.

It was the law.

It took me a while to find out why Tom had been arrested in our home that night, mainly because none of the officers I screamed at as he was led out of the door in handcuffs were able to give me any more information at the time. But I did find out a few hours later at the police station, and when I did, my whole world came crashing down.

I knew that Tom had been arrested for murder, but I didn't know who the victim was. That was until PC Brown gave me the name.

Jesse Addams.

My last boyfriend was dead, joining all my other exes in the afterlife. He had been stabbed to death in his own home, a violent and brutal murder, even worse than how Ash was killed. It was clear that the killer had given up the secrecy and disguise that they had started with, progressing from faking suicides to stabbing and slashing.

But now it seemed to be over.

I had no more exes left.

I didn't want to believe that Tom was the one behind all of this. I told PC Brown that there had to be some kind of mistake, even though the fact that Tom had cuts and bruises on his body seemed to suggest that he had been involved in a violent attack recently, which could have been with either Ash, Jesse, or both. And I pointed out that the last message I received from the mystery number had told me that Tom's turn was coming.

But then PC Brown gave me the evidence they had on my fiancé. It was damning. There was camera phone footage of Tom at Jesse's flat on the night the latter was killed. A neighbour had taken it from their bedroom window after hearing an altercation outside and looked out to see the two men arguing on Jesse's doorstep. Then Tom had forced his way inside and closed the door. The neighbour had waited to see what happened and was able to film Tom leaving four minutes later. It was only when Jesse's current partner got home a few hours later that she found his body and called the police. The sight of the body bag being carried from the house made the neighbour realise that the video she had on her phone wasn't just something interesting she could show to her friends at work the next day.

It was potentially evidence of the last few moments of Jesse Addams' life.

And it was Tom who was the last person to be seen with him before he died.

PC Brown was right when he shook his head and told me that it didn't look good.

It didn't look good for Tom.

And it didn't look good for me.

## 31

My migraines are back, although I surely can't put these down to that incident in my teenage years when I banged my head and woke up in hospital. This time, it could simply be down to all the stress that I am under after seeing my fiancé taken away in handcuffs before being told that he was the prime suspect in the murder of my last boyfriend. But I don't have time to go and lie down in a dark room like I usually do when the migraines strike. There's another knock at my door, which has to be answered, even though the last thing I want to do right now is see another human being.

As I walk into the hallway, I try to figure out who it could be this time. Maybe my parents coming around again to check on me. They've already been around three times since I told them what was happening with Tom, but they might have come back to make sure that I'm okay. I wouldn't blame them if they had because I am definitely not okay. They tried to convince me to stay with them for a few days, but I refused, so perhaps they've come back to have another try.

Or maybe it's Nicola calling around again with another bottle of wine, ready to lend another listening ear or a shoulder to cry on. We've spent a few hours together since Tom was taken away, and most of it consisted of me gulping wine down in between bursts of tears. I doubt it has been much fun for her, but she is my loyal pal, so I guess she is willing to go through it all just to help me feel better.

But then I reach the door and see the shape behind the frosted glass, and I know that it doesn't belong to either of my parents or my best friend.

There's a tall man out there.

I just don't know who it is.

After everything that has happened, my initial reaction is to be cautious and not open my door to anybody I'm not expecting, so I pause with my hand on the latch.

'Who is it?' I call out, wondering if the person is going to give me an honest answer.

'It's Detective Inspector Rodgers. I'm here with PC Brown, whom I believe you have been speaking with at the station. Can we come inside?'

The appearance of a detective on my doorstep cannot be a good thing, and part of me wants to refuse simply because I don't feel like I can handle any more bad news right now. My head is banging, so the thought of having to go through pleasantries with a policeman is not an appealing one. But the fact that he mentioned PC Brown is ultimately why I decide to open my door – despite the police officer's initial scepticism when I first reported my fears, he has since been nothing but a big help to me.

Opening the door, I see the familiar face of PC Brown before getting a look at the man he is with. Like I saw through the frosted glass, Detective Rodgers is a tall man, possibly even as tall as six feet five, and his smartly cut hair and designer stubble makes me wonder why he went into this line of work instead of modelling. It would surely pay more, and he wouldn't have to make doorstep visits to distressed fiancées at all hours of the day.

'What's happened now?' I ask. I've had so much bad news recently that it's got to the point where it's all I expect to hear anymore.

'Could we come inside?' Detective Rodgers asks with a grave look of concern on his chiselled face. 'We have some news about your ex-boyfriends.'

I step aside and let the two men in, and thirty seconds later, we are seated at my kitchen table. I didn't take them into the living room because I didn't want them to see all the empty wine bottles and take-away boxes, although the kitchen isn't much better. It doesn't smell too good, and I'm sure something is rotting in the fridge, but I haven't investigated – household chores have been the last thing on my to-do list recently.

'As you are aware, we have been looking into the deaths of your former boyfriends, as you requested with PC Brown on several occasions over the last few weeks,' Detective Rodgers begins. 'At the time, we believed the death of Calum Jenkins to have been the result of a tragic but non-suspicious car accident. But the full report from that incident has now been completed, and it is evident that the brakes were tampered with before the crash.'

It's something that I suspected for a long time, but hearing it told to me by a detective is sobering, and I take a few seconds to gather my thoughts.

'What does that mean?' I ask. I already know the answer – I just want to hear this man say it.

'It would appear that somebody wanted Calum to

crash and did what they could to make that happen,' the detective tells me.

I nod, but I don't feel much better for being vindicated. I'm wondering if they think the person who tampered with those brakes was my fiancé.

'That's not all,' Detective Rodgers says. 'We were also able to gain the cooperation of the authorities in Portsmouth who were looking into the house fire in which Ryan Harris lost his life. That too had been treated as non-suspicious, but after PC Brown's diligent work in getting them to look into it further, it has been determined that the electrical appliance that was originally deemed to be faulty had also been tampered with.'

I glance at PC Brown, who is now looking at me as a victim rather than the nuisance he met the first time we ever spoke. It must be the sight of the sympathy in his eyes that causes the tears to suddenly flow from my own.

As PC Brown grabs a box of tissues for me, Detective Rodgers gives me a few moments to get my emotions in check, and I'm grateful that both of these men are handling me with care right now because it's taking all my restraint not to slide out of my seat and onto the kitchen floor.

'Do you think Tom did all of that?' I ask after wiping my eyes several times and going through half a box of tissues.

'That's what we are trying to determine,' Detective Rodgers says. 'But we need your help.'

'What do you mean?'

'If Tom did kill Ryan, it meant he had to travel down south and back again around the time of the fire. The blaze was reported at nine p.m. on the evening of Wednesday the sixteenth of May. Do you recall your partner's whereabouts on that day?'

'Can't you just ask him?'

'We did, and he gave us an answer that we are working to corroborate. But we would like to know where you believed he was at the time.'

I do my best to recall the date, but with everything that's happened recently, and with my buzz saw of a migraine, I'm struggling to think back to that day.

'I don't know. I'd have to look at my messages. I might have texts from him that day telling me what he was doing if he was out.'

'If you could check those for us, that would be great.'

I realise he means that he wants me to do it now, so I get up from the table and head into the living room in search of my phone. As I'm accessing my device, the tears return, but this time, I can't control them as well. I drop to my knees as waves of emotion roll over me. I'm having to look for something that will prove my fiancé's innocence – but the very fact that it's being questioned by a detective in my own home is worrying.

The two men in my kitchen must have heard my sobbing because they both rush into the living room and come to my assistance, helping me up onto one of the sofas and accidentally knocking off an empty pizza box as they do. Even in my distress, I'm able to feel a touch of embarrassment because they have seen the squalor I have been living in since Tom got taken into custody two days ago, and I hate it. I hate it because this is not the kind of person I am. I don't usually burst into tears every ten minutes or survive on a diet of bad pizza and cheap wine.

I'm strong. I'm experienced. I have responsibilities. I was supposed to be getting married.

But what do I have now? Just two men trying to console me as they try to find out if the man whom I love is a serial killer.

I should pull myself together. I should be stronger than this. After what Jesse did to me, I thought I was. But this is even worse.

I feel like giving up. At least four of my exes were definitely murdered, and it sounds like Tom is the only suspect.

What's the point of anything anymore? How could I ever trust another man again?

Forget the white wedding.

I can't see how I can live with this.

## 32

## THE BOYFRIEND

I can see plenty from where I am standing right now. I can see into the kitchen because the blinds are still open over the window. I can see the messy countertops inside littered with dirty plates and empty milk cartons. And I can see the homeowner every time she moves past that window and walks around the room, tidying up or at least attempting to.

But she looks distracted.

Sad.

Most importantly, she looks alone.

I have been standing outside Adele's house for the past hour, watching her move around inside from my vantage point in her back garden. I'm not worried about her spotting me out here. It's too dark for that, and I'm well hidden enough by the exterior of the garden shed.

She can't see me.

But I can see her.

*My only wish is that I could get closer to her. Alas, that is not an option. I'm not going to break in, and I'm certainly not going to knock on the back door. I'll just have to be content with catching glimpses of her through that kitchen window.*

*This will have to be close enough.*

*For now.*

*Adele disappears from view again, and I hope she is still in the kitchen rather than having gone somewhere else in the house because that would make it harder for me to keep an eye on her. But then I hear the sound of a door unlocking, and I realise that she is coming out into the garden.*

*Squeezing myself further down the side of the shed, I make sure to stay out of view of her as she leaves her house, clutching a full bin bag in her hand. The light filtering through the kitchen window gives me a good look at her face as she passes by the shed, and I see that she looks exhausted. But then she disappears from view, going down the side of the house, presumably because that's where she keeps the bins.*

*I plan on remaining in my safe hiding place until she has gone back inside the house. But then I can't help noticing the tempting invitation right before me.*

*The back door is wide open.*

*I'm out of my hiding place before I've even had time to think about what I'm doing, rushing towards the open door and stepping inside before heading deeper into the vacant home. I hear the sound of the bin lid closing outside as I head for the stairs, excited and nervous in equal measure at what I am doing. Being in Adele's house is thrilling, but getting caught here would be dangerous for my plan.*

*I'll just have to make sure I don't get caught then.*

*Rushing up the staircase, I go into the first door I see, which seems to be the master bedroom. I see one of Adele's blouses on the bed, and I long to pick it up and detect her scent, but I leave it where it is and keep exploring. Leaving the bedroom, I go into the next room. Another bedroom, this one* much smaller. I guess it's the spare room, and I assume there won't be much of interest in here for me.

But I'm wrong.

I stare at the item on the shelf, feeling those familiar feelings of frustration bubbling up again in my body.

I should get out of here. It's already been too long. But I'm distracted by what I have seen.

And then I hear the back door closing downstairs.

## 33

I feel the chill in the evening air as I hurry down the side of the house towards where the bins are kept. It should be warmer than this with summer on the horizon, but I have a feeling that I'm not going to be able to enjoy that particular season for a long time. It was the season when all my dreams were supposed to come true, when I would have married Tom and celebrated with all our family and friends at a beautiful venue before we embarked on the holiday of a lifetime. But now those plans are in ruins, as useless as all the rubbish in this bin bag as I toss it into the bin and turn back to the house.

As I re-enter the kitchen, I close the back door but leave it unlocked because I plan on filling several bin bags tonight before I'm done. Now that I've started with the cleaning, I feel like I can't stop, and while it might only be a temporary distraction, I'm willing to milk it for as long as I can.

They say it's always darkest before the dawn. I have to cling to the hope there is going to be some light on the horizon because right now, I can't possibly see how things can get any worse. After being overwhelmed by my emotions during the visit of the detective, I was able to get myself together enough to go through my messages and try to recall where Tom had been the night when Ryan died. Detective Rodgers told me that Tom was using a work conference as his alibi, and witnesses were being questioned to ensure that he was really in attendance and not elsewhere. But before that, there is still the camera footage of Tom at Jesse's home on the night he died, along with the cuts and bruises, so things are looking decidedly bleak for my fiancé.

Yet he is denying all charges and maintaining his innocence, and I'm still hoping that the police have got this wrong and he is not the person they are looking for. But the evidence is not looking good for him, and the only options are that he is guilty, or he's innocent and has been in the wrong place at the wrong time at least twice.

Like Jesse's home, for instance. Detective Rodgers has told me that Tom's explanation for being there, while not entirely honourable, was not because he planned to kill the man. He had gone there after learning how Jesse had treated me in the past, tracking him down based on the address I had given to PC Brown when we were together at the police station, and intending to punish Jesse for his violence towards me years ago. While that makes him guilty of assault and threatening behaviour, it doesn't make him a murderer, and Tom is adamant that Jesse was still alive when he left his property that night.

The trouble for the police, and indeed for me, is that the timeline is almost too coincidental if Tom is telling the truth. What are the chances that somebody else visited Jesse with the intention of doing him harm on the same night that Tom did? As much as I love my fiancé and want him to be innocent, even I have to admit that I'm having a hard time believing that Jesse was attacked by two different people on the same night.

But there is a chance, and the police are still unsure if Tom really is the killer they are looking for. There's also the message on my phone in which Tom was clearly counted as being a target just like my ex-boyfriends. Unless, of course, Tom was the person who sent that message and wrote it in a way that might deflect suspicion from him.

It's all a mess, and nobody knows what to believe. Not me. Not the police. And not the rest of the people in this town, who are no doubt reading about it all in the newspapers and gossiping over their breakfasts and evening meals.

I hate to think that everybody is talking about me and my relationships as if I'm some character in a soap opera and not a real person who is trying her best, but there is no doubt that they are. Blackburn isn't exactly the murder capital of England, so the fact that there has been so much going on here lately means it's impossible for it to not be the talk of the town. And while it is Tom's name being spoken about as the guilty party, my name will always be linked to his and my past used as the motive to explain the reasoning behind the murders. The poor murder victims can't be brought be back either, meaning there will always be a black cloud hanging over this town now thanks to its connection to a grim past.

I'm sure I'd be forgiven for crawling into bed and hiding under my duvet until all of this was over and the people of the town had moved on with their lives, but I know I can't do that. Life doesn't work that way, and my migraine has eased off, so I'm feeling well enough to be a little more productive than closing my eyes and escaping into the darkness. The first job on my list is to clean the living room of all the takeaway boxes and wine bottles.

It's already too late for them not to be seen by Detective Rodgers and PC Brown, but I can at least get rid of them before I have any more visitors – it's only a matter of time until my parents or Nicola call around again. And I know that having a tidy-up, even a quick one, will make me feel like I've done something productive.

Heading up the stairs and into my bedroom with a roll of bin bags in one hand and a feather duster in the other, I'm doing a surprisingly good job of forgetting about my troubles – until I hear a floorboard creaking in the room next to this one.

I pause and listen out for it again, feeling the fear that comes when you hear a noise, but you're the only person in the house. I don't hear any more sounds, which makes me think it was nothing sinister and just the house settling, so I go back to my dusting and tidying.

Then I hear the sound of glass shattering in the spare bedroom.

With no windows open anywhere, there's no way that could have been caused by anything other than somebody else being in the house.

*I'm not alone.*

I think about calling out, but my voice catches in my throat, and I'm too gripped by fear to do anything other than creep towards the en-suite door, prepared to rush inside and lock myself in should I need to.

For a second, I have a brief moment of hope that my mobile phone is in my pocket, which would let me call for help and hopefully scare off the intruder, but it's not there. Then I remember that I left it on the kitchen table.

*I have no way of calling for help.*

As I stand in the doorway to my bathroom and listen out, I hear no more noises. Whoever it is out there, they aren't coming for me.

Not yet, anyway.

Realising that I can't stay like this all night, I take several deep breaths before mustering up the courage to call out.

'Hello?' I cry, although I'm not sure if getting a response would be a good or a bad thing. 'Who's there?'

There's no reply, but I know the person is still here because I haven't heard any more sounds since the glass broke a moment ago.

'I'm calling the police! You'd better leave now!'

I hope that I was convincing, but I'm doubtful. The fact that I hear no sound of the intruder making their escape only proves my fears right. I'm not doing a very good job of scaring them off.

*I'm clearly the only one who is scared here.*

I don't know what to do, but it seems I only have two choices. Hide in this bathroom or go out and investigate. Neither appeals to me for very different reasons, but if I lock myself in here, I will be completely cornered and powerless to stop whatever the intruder is doing. At least if I go out, then I might have a chance of scaring him off because I've spent long enough being afraid of this person.

It takes all my willpower to force myself out of the bathroom. But as I reach the bedroom door and look out, I see a hooded figure dash out of the spare bedroom and run down the stairs, their speed taking me by surprise.

'Hey!' I call after them, but they're already gone, and a second later, I hear the sound of the back door opening.

Adrenaline has taken over from the fear now, and I

run down the stairs in pursuit, desperate to know who it was who just broke in. But the sight of the open back door lets me know that they are gone, and after a few seconds looking out into the dark garden, I quickly lock the door in case they return.

Grabbing my phone, I call the police and tell them about the intruder, and they promise me that they will have somebody round as soon as they can. As I wait for the police to visit my home for what would be the second time in twenty-four hours, I go back upstairs to check on the damage from the broken glass. I assume it came from the window, but to my surprise, the window is still intact, and there are no signs of forced entry or exit there.

Looking around the spare bedroom, it takes me a moment to figure out what it was that was smashed. But then I see it.

It's the photo frame on the shelf.

The frame that holds a picture from my past.

It's the photo of all the final-year pupils from my secondary school, taken when we were sixteen and just about to leave. I kept it as a nice memory, as well as the fact that it's funny to look back at it and see what the people I'm still in touch with today looked like back then.

There are over fifty students in the photo, including myself, Nicola, Rachel, and Shaun, who is standing right behind me in the image with one hand on my shoulder. But now the frame is broken and the glass cracked, turning a happy and innocent image into a damaged and unsettling one.

Why did the intruder smash this picture?

*Is the past connected to what's happening now?*

I 'm sitting opposite a policeman again, but that's not the only reason I have the feeling of déjà vu. Just like I spent so long having to convince PC Brown to take me seriously, I'm having to try to convince this new officer that what I am telling him is the truth.

He seems unsure about my claims that there was an intruder in my house this evening. There are no signs of forced entry anywhere, nor any other clues that suggest that anybody other than me has been here tonight.

'He must have got in when I took the rubbish out,' I say, having figured out that the only way the intruder could have accessed my home was through the unlocked back door when I was outside.

'Why would somebody break in while you were home?' the officer, who introduced himself as PC Giles, asks me as he continues to furrow his brow and look at me like I'm the most annoying thing to happen to his night shift in a long time.

'I don't know. To scare me, maybe?' I suggest.

'Can you think of any reason why anybody would want to do that?'

'No, but they obviously wanted me to know that they were here. Why else would they smash the photo frame in my spare bedroom?'

PC Giles takes another look at the damaged frame lying on the coffee table nearby.

'It definitely couldn't have just fallen onto the floor?'

'No. They smashed it. And then I saw them run down the stairs.'

I feel like I'm going round in circles because I've already told the policeman this three times since he entered my home, but he still seems to be having a hard time grasping it. It's only then that he reveals why.

'I understand your partner is currently in police custody,' he says, glancing at one of the photos on the mantelpiece that show Tom and me in happier times.

'That's right.'

'I imagine that is very difficult for you.'

I pause because I'm not sure what he means by that. Is he insinuating that I somehow imagined this whole thing? If so, I'm about to give him a piece of my mind.

He must be able to sense that because he quickly speaks again.

'We've got officers in the area on the lookout for anybody matching the description you gave us. If they're out there, we will find them.'

I nod my head, although I'm not hopeful on their search bearing much fruit. All I saw was the glimpse of a figure dressed in black with a hood preventing me from getting a look at their face. They can hardly draw up an e-fit from that.

'What if this is connected to everything that's been going on?' I say before PC Giles can get up to leave.

'How do you mean?'

'Well, what if the person who broke in here tonight is

actually the one who is responsible for the murders of my ex-boyfriends?'

That's a question that is clearly beyond the brain-power of the man opposite me because he just scratches his head and clearly has no answer.

'That could be why they didn't take anything,' I add. 'They weren't looking to steal. They were looking to scare me. And it's worked.'

'Look, I can try to get Detective Rodgers to give you a call if you think this is in some way connected to his investigation.'

'Yes, please do that,' I say, aware that I'd be much better off speaking to the man in charge and not just some weary police officer who probably just wants to finish his late shift and go home.

After assuring PC Giles that I'm okay to stay in my own home this evening, I close the door on him, and it's a relief to have him out of the house. I need time to think, and I haven't had a lot of that since I first found out somebody had sneaked into my house.

Returning to the sofa, I think about the possibility of the intruder being the person behind all of the terrible things that have happened recently. If that is the case, Tom is innocent, at least of the more serious crime of murder. He still has some explaining to do for the assault of Jesse, but he says he only did that in my honour. But I'll have to see what Detective Rodgers thinks of all this.

I also think about the significance of the broken photo frame. Clearly, whoever was here tonight did not intend to do me any harm – they could have easily done so if they had just gone for me, but it seems obvious that the sight of the school photo infuriated them somewhat.

But why? What is the significance of that time in my life?

I pick the photo up and take a look at all the rows of faces within it. Everybody looks so young and fresh-faced. Of course they do; this was taken when we were all full of youth and vigour, eager to finish school and make our mark on the world. In hindsight, I know that most of the people in this image didn't make it much further than Blackburn, and the fact I was able to talk to so many of them at Shaun's funeral let me know that while they are all living more than adequate lifestyles, they have hardly set the world alight in the last twenty years. Neither have I, although I am certainly famous enough now to be the talk of the town, thanks to the fact that all my exes have died, and my fiancé is in custody on suspicion of their murders.

But then a thought hits me so suddenly that I'm amazed I hadn't thought of it sooner. What if the person who came into my home tonight and broke this photo frame is *one of the people in this picture*? Is that why the sight of it elicited such a strong emotion from them? And is all of this, my exes, the murders and the messages, somehow linked to this time in my life?

Sixteen. The final year of school.

*The year I had the accident.*

The photo falls from my hand and onto the carpet as I realise everything that is happening now could be a consequence of something that happened two decades ago. But now that I have that thought, so much makes sense. The killer has to be someone who knows about my relationship history, and it could very well be some-body I have known since I was sixteen, especially if I still have them on social media now.

Does one of my old classmates have some kind of vendetta against me? Or is he obsessed with me and has followed my life ever since I left school?

I have no idea, but I need to voice my theory with Detective Rodgers, and I need to do it now.

Grabbing the photo from where it fell onto the carpet, I rush for the door, pulling on my coat before heading outside and getting behind the wheel of my car. It's late now, almost midnight, but there was no chance I was ever going to be able to sleep anyway after all the drama, so I'm hardly going to worry about being up all night. But the longer this mystery remains unsolved, the longer Tom remains in custody, and after seeing the intruder tonight, I'm convinced now that he is innocent.

The intruder is the guilty party. I just know it, and I believe the person may be in the school photo that is lying on the seat beside me.

The question is, who? And can I help catch them before they come back?

Because next time, they might not run away.

## 35

I never made it to the police station that night. I had to turn back halfway because I had another migraine come on, and this one was so sudden and so severe that the thought of sitting in a bright police station talking to a detective was the last thing I needed. Fortunately, I was able to make it back home, although I had to drive very slowly in doing so with one hand on the wheel and one on my throbbing head. Now I'm in my bedroom with the lights off and my eyes closed, but the pain in my skull isn't easing off yet.

This is one of the bad ones, the kind I only get once or twice a year. Unlike the milder migraines, which have occurred once a week or so ever since my accident and can generally be relieved by an hour somewhere dark and quiet, these are the kind that have me feeling as if I want somebody to drill into my head and release the pressure in there. It's almost ironic because these migraines are a consequence of a night I can't remember, yet I have no chance of ever forgetting it because I end up crippled by the headaches on a regular basis. If I knew what had happened to me that night in the park when I was sixteen, then I might be able to understand all this better. As it is, I have spent the last twenty years having to manage these lingering symptoms while still none the wiser as to how I ended up with a head injury in the first place.

But after tonight with the intruder and the broken school photo, I need to have another go at remembering.

I can't hope to have much luck tonight with the way I'm feeling now, but as soon as this migraine subsides, then I am going to contact the therapist I saw twenty years ago and see if she can have another go at helping me unlock the memory from that incident in my past. The therapist's name was Dr Wendy Armitage, and I know she still has her own clinic because I follow her business on social media, although I haven't had a session with her since my early twenties. That was when I had just finished university and was thinking about going travelling. But before I did, I decided that I wanted to have another go at seeing if she could help me remember that night when I was sixteen. Sadly, just like all the other times we had tried it, nothing came of it. I still couldn't recall what I was doing in that park and whom I might have been with.

But I will contact Wendy in the morning and make an appointment. I have to try, on the chance that everything that is happening now could be linked to that mystery, even though I doubt anything will be different. Surely if I was going to remember, I would have done so by now. It certainly wasn't for a lack of trying on Wendy's part. She went to great lengths to make sure that I was always as comfortable as I could possibly be when I was in a session with her, and never pushed me further than I wanted to go at the time. But looking back, maybe that's what the problem was. Maybe she didn't push me enough, and maybe I didn't force more out of myself to recover those memories. Perhaps I didn't want it enough and lacked real motivation. I admit there was a part of me that was a little scared of remembering in case there was a memory that would have terrified me. That part of me is still there. But now I have more of an urgent reason to try to unlock that forgotten night. It might be the only way I can solve the mystery of what is happening now.

I don't just want to remember anymore.

I think I need to.

## 36

I f I needed any more motivation to get myself to Wendy's office and in another of her therapy sessions, I got it the very next morning before I could even give her a call. I was woken up by the sound of the front door opening, and when I rushed out of the bedroom, I saw Tom standing at the bottom of the stairs, looking up at me with a tired look on his face.

'What's happened?' I ask him, wanting to rush down and welcome him home, but I'm not clear why he is here. When I went to bed, he was still in police custody under investigation for murder. So I'm wondering why he is suddenly home, looking like he is ready to crawl in bed.

'They let me go. Murder charges are dropped,' he tells me, although he's not smiling as he speaks. 'They're still deciding what to do about my assault on Jesse, but they know now that I wasn't the one who killed him or any of those other guys.'

'They do?'

The question is out of my mouth before I can stop it, but I wish I had because it obviously suggests I'm surprised by this turn of events, which I am, although I shouldn't be showing it. I should be running down these stairs and wrapping my arms around my fiancé, so that's what I quickly decide to do.

I reach the bottom of the stairs and hug Tom, and while I can feel that he's not being overly warm towards me, he does hug me back, and it feels good.

'I'm so sorry all of this has happened,' I tell him after giving him a kiss.

'That makes two of us.'

I decide to give us both a distraction as quickly as possible. 'Can I get you anything? Breakfast?'

'A coffee would be good.'

I smile as I lead Tom into the kitchen, and he eases himself into a seat at the table as I hurry around and make him a cup of caffeine.

'So what happened, then?' I ask him when the kettle has finally boiled.

'My alibis stood up, and my phone records showed I hadn't been anywhere near the places where Calum, Ryan, or Ash were killed.'

'And what about Jesse?'

'A witness has come forward to say that they saw somebody else go to his property that night, not long after I left.'

'Who?'

Tom shrugs. 'They don't know yet. But it's created enough doubt for them to let me go. There's not enough evidence to hold me anymore.'

'That's great!' I say, although the fact I even have to celebrate it tells me how close I was to believing that Tom might actually have been behind this.

He obviously picks up on that because he barely smiles at my reaction, and I can see we have some serious bridges to mend. But I'm confident we can do that. It will certainly be much easier to get back on track without him being a murder suspect.

I deliver the cup of coffee to my fiancé before returning to the kitchen counter and popping a couple of slices of bread into the toaster. It's only now I am handling food that I realise I haven't eaten in over a day. By the look of Tom, he might be able to say the same thing, although I'm sure they did give him meals in custody.

'So what? They just dropped you off here and are leaving us to it?'

'I guess,' Tom says with a shrug before taking a sip of his coffee. I suspect it might be a little too hot for him yet, but he doesn't even flinch as he takes a drink. He wasn't lying when he said he needed it. But I've got bigger worries now. When Tom was in custody, he was safe from any potential attacker on the outside. Now that he's home and the police are looking for other suspects, he's vulnerable again.

I feel another migraine coming on, or maybe it's still the remnants of my last one, but whatever it is, I put my hand to my head and do my best to try to stay calm.

'Adele, what's wrong?' Tom asks, reaching out for my arm, and it's clear that he's either too tired to be as worried as I am or just relieved to be out of custody and happy to be sitting in his kitchen again. But I'm guessing he won't be so relaxed when I tell him what happened while he was away.

'Somebody broke in here last night.'

'What? How?'

'Through the back door. I heard them in the spare bedroom. They smashed one of my old school photos.'

'Oh, my god,' Tom says, and now he finally looks alive, jumping up out of his seat and checking to make sure that I'm okay. 'What did you do?'

'I chased them out.'

'You did what?'

'I guess it was the adrenaline. I don't know. I just really wanted to see who it was.'

'And did you?'

I shake my head. 'But I figure it must have been the person who has been doing all of this, right?'

Tom thinks about it for a moment before nodding. 'Yeah, I guess.'

The burning smell from the toaster suggests we need to check on it, but neither of us are making a move to.

'This is ridiculous. We shouldn't be here,' Tom says, his thrill at being home fading fast now that he realises this isn't over yet. 'We need to go and stay somewhere else until they catch whoever it is.'

I suspect he is right, but I really don't want to have to leave. I'd rather the police were keeping guard outside the property, but it doesn't seem like that is happening, so maybe we have to take measures ourselves. It's funny, but I almost felt safer being here by myself rather than now when Tom is present. It's not my safety I'm worried about. It's his. Even though the mystery intruder ran away after startling me yesterday, I have a feeling that they wouldn't have run if Tom had been home.

*They would have hurt him.*

'Where shall we go?' I ask him.

'I don't know. A hotel, maybe. Or I could ask my parents,' Tom suggests.

I think about both of those options, but the thought of being cooped up in a small hotel room or at Tom's parents is not appealing. I briefly consider suggesting my parents' place because it's a big country house set behind a large security gate, so we would not only be safe there but have plenty of space to ourselves. But I don't want to put them at risk if anything bad is going to happen and somebody might come for us.

The sound of the toast popping up behind me causes both of us to jump, and we turn around to see the two blackened pieces of bread sticking out of the toaster, smoke floating off the top of them.

We both laugh nervously at the fact that the toaster startled us, and it feels good to relieve a little bit of tension, even if breakfast is ruined. But it's the simple comfort of being in my own home with my fiancé by my side again that makes me decide what we should do.

'Before we go anywhere, there's something I want to try,' I tell him. 'I want to try the therapist again and see if she can help me remember what happened when I was sixteen.'

Tom looks troubled by that, but I guess only because he knows how frustrated I got with it not working before.

'You think it has something to do with this?'

'I do,' I reply, nodding my head and becoming more sure of it by the hour. 'It makes sense. The broken school photo. The fact that they have known everything about me. It has to be connected to my past, and that's the only part I can't recall.'

Tom takes a deep breath, and I can see that he's still not convinced, but only because he is probably worried about me dredging up something that might be painful for me.

'We have to try something,' I say, taking his hands and holding them tightly. 'Because I can't lose you. I just can't.'

'You really think that therapist will be able to help you this time?'

The honest answer is no, simply because she has never been able to help me before. But I also know that she has the best chance out of anybody because she has already done so much work with me.

'I don't know,' I reply with a shrug. 'But we have to try everything, don't we? Because I can't lose you, and I can't let that killer get away with murder.'

## 37

It feels weird being back here again. Some things about this office have never changed. Like the squeaky toilet door just off the waiting room. Or the strange painting behind the receptionist's desk that I'm sure is expensive and artistic but always confused me. Or the clock on the wall to my left with the loud second hand ticking round and round and round, reminding everybody who sits in this room that it is only a matter of time until it stops ticking for us all.

The first time I came to Dr Armitage's office, I was sixteen years old and had just spent over a month recovering at home after the blow to my head had landed me in hospital. It had been apparent back then that while I was making a speedy recovery physically, I was still nowhere near being able to recall what had happened that night. That was why I was referred to this office, and I remember feeling confident that this was going to work when I sat here that first time. Dr Armitage was the best in her field, I was told. She helps people remember all kinds of things, so surely she would be able to help me too. She's friendly, polite, and a great listener.

All of those things turned out to be true, except one.

She wasn't able to make me remember.

Despite how lovely the therapist was, or how much I knew she was doing as good a job as anybody, she wasn't able to help me remember how I banged my head. The more I came back and sat in this waiting room, the less confident I began to feel about ever remembering, and that was why my visits became less frequent over the years before I eventually stopped coming at all. But now I'm back, even though I can't help thinking that nothing will have changed. Why should it have? The squeaky door is the same. So too the weird painting and the loud clock. And my brain is the same. A little older, yes, but still the same. Same memories. Same experiences. Same problem trying to retrieve them.

At least Tom is with me this time. He has never been here before and only knows about this place because I told him about it a few times over dinner, but now he is getting to experience a place that made up a big part of my youth. While all my friends were out having fun at sixteen, drinking illegally and snogging boys behind the bike sheds, I spent many a night sitting here after school, hoping to get my memory back so I could fill in the one missing puzzle piece of my young life.

'Adele, how lovely to see you!'

I jump a little in my seat, surprised by the sound of Dr Armitage's voice over my shoulder. I didn't hear her office door open, although it was always much quieter than the bathroom one. Turning around, I see the familiar face smiling back at me, and while the one memory I am desperate to unlock still eludes me, the sight of her does bring back plenty of other ones.

'Hi,' I say, getting up out of my seat and moving to shake the woman's hand. I notice Tom stand up awkwardly beside me and realise I should make the necessary introductions.

'Dr Armitage, this is my fiancé, Tom.'

'Come on, you know better than that,' the therapist says, waving her hand in the air dismissively. 'It's Wendy when you're with me.'

I smile because I know she is right. She always insisted on me calling her by her first name and not her professional one, and I guess that's just one more thing around here that hasn't changed.

'Your fiancé. Wow, you have grown up, haven't you?' Wendy says with a chuckle before shaking Tom's hand.

'Nice to meet you,' he says ever so politely, although he seems a little awkward to me, and I'm not sure if it's just because he is shy or because he thinks this is a waste of time and not a cheap one at that.

When I first started coming here, these sessions were free, provided by that wonderful thing called the NHS and considered a vital part of my recovery. But then there were changes, and my mum had to start paying for it, which she was happy to do but only made me feel under more pressure to remember something about that night. When I was older, I started paying for myself, but with no progress being made, I decided that I could put that money to better use on things like holidays and happy hours. But it's not just the cost of these sessions that saw me stop coming here. It's that I will have to spend an hour taking myself back to a time when I felt scared and vulnerable in my life, yet not getting anything positive from it when the memory fails to return.

I know that it is not Wendy's fault. She really is the

best in her field. Some patients are trickier than others, and I know that I am one of her trickiest ones because she has admitted that to me before. But who knows? Maybe today will be different. I am desperate to recall my memory, perhaps more desperate than ever. Recalling that night might not just explain what happened to me and help me find out if anybody was to blame for the injury I suffered. It could also protect Tom from the person who might be coming for him next.

I'm glad to have him here with me, where I can see that he is safe. But as we follow Wendy towards her office, she suddenly stops in the doorway and looks back at us both apologetically.

'I'm sorry, but all my sessions are one-on-one these days,' she says, clearly hinting that Tom isn't going to be allowed to sit in on this appointment with us.

'Oh, okay,' I say, feeling slightly awkward. My mum used to sit in on these with me in the past, so I had assumed Tom would have been okay to do the same thing.

'Sorry, I've just found it produces better results than the old way,' Wendy adds, and I'm not going to disagree with somebody way more qualified than I am.

'You don't mind waiting here, do you?' I ask Tom, and while he doesn't look thrilled by the prospect of having to stay back in the waiting room on his own for the next hour, he doesn't really have much choice.

'Yeah, sure,' he mumbles before heading back to his seat, destined to have to listen to that squeaky door and ticking clock for the next sixty minutes.

I feel slightly anxious to be leaving him behind as I enter Wendy's office and she closes the door, even though I know anything bad is unlikely to happen to him here. But there is still somebody out there wishing to do him harm, so every second he is out of my sight is a second when my imagination can run wild.

'Just take a seat on the chair,' Wendy tells me, and she goes around to the other side of her desk and picks up a piece of paper, which I presume has my notes on it. It has been a while since I've been here, and I assume she has seen thousands of people in amongst my appointments, so I can hardly blame her for needing a little reminder. But it's not her memory that needs jogging.

It's mine.

'So I can see that it's been a long time since your last appointment with me,' she says as I settle into the comfortable chair, and she walks around to take her seat in the one beside me. 'Is there any particular reason you have decided to give this another go, other than wanting to know what happened?'

I consider being coy with my answer and just telling her that I thought it might be worth another shot. But then I remember something she told me on one of my very first appointments twenty years ago. She told me how important it was that I was honest with her at all times because the more information I could give her, the better chance she had of helping me. With that in mind, I decide to be straight.

'My fiancé is in danger,' I begin, trying to keep myself calm because I know that is important for what is to come in this next hour. 'Somebody is threatening us. They have sent messages, they broke into our home, and they have killed my ex-boyfriends. I think whoever is doing all of this is someone who knew me when I was at school. It might even be connected to whatever happened to me that night when I banged my head. Basically, the police have no idea who it is, and I don't know either, but if I don't come up with something soon, then I think Tom is going to be next.'

Wendy stares back at me with her jaw hanging open, and for a second, I worry that I've been too honest. But then, like a true pro, she regains her composure and clears her throat.

'I guess we'd better make a start, then.'

## 38

Wendy started the session like she always liked to do, running me through a series of breathing exercises designed to make me calm and more receptive for what was to come. As I inhaled through my nose and exhaled through my mouth, I wondered if the fact that everything seemed so similar meant that the end result was going to be the same. But ten minutes later, Wendy took a detour from the way she usually did things, which gave me optimism that this time the outcome could be different.

'There's a new technique I've been having some success with recently, and I was wondering if you would like to give it a try,' she says to me as I keep my eyes closed and my breathing steady. 'It's slightly different from what we have done before, but I think it could be useful in this case. Are you willing to give it a go?'

I don't hesitate and nod to let her know that I am.

'Okay, first of all, I need you to hold out your hands in front of you.'

I do as I'm told, lifting my arms and feeling as if they

are suddenly much heavier than normal. But this always used to happen whenever I was here. Wendy would put me in such a relaxed state that I felt as if I were sinking deeper into myself, and every movement after that felt more difficult, as if my mind were going somewhere else and my body were being left behind to fend for itself.

'Can you feel my touch?' Wendy asks as she takes hold of my hands, and I nod again.

'I want you to try to pull them away from me if you can.'

I do as she tells me and can feel her pulling in the opposite way to prevent it, though it's not painful.

'Now push your hands against mine,' she says, and I respond in kind, feeling the different kind of pressure that comes with that change in movement.

'Good, now let your hands relax again.'

I lower my arms and rest my hands in my lap, and it feels nice to do so. I'm not sure what the relevance of the exercise was, or if it will be in any way helpful, but I guess I'll find out soon enough. All I know is that I feel more relaxed than any other time I have been here.

'What did you do on the day of your accident?' Wendy asks, and the question surprises me a little, mainly because she asked me it in my very first session, so she already knows the answer.

'I went to school,' I reply, and a vision of that old building where I spent so many years comes into my mind. I can see the uniforms. I can see the playground. And I can hear that damn bell ringing to let me know that another class is about to begin.

'What did you do after school?'

'I went home. I watched TV. My dad was there. He had finished work early.'

'What did you talk about?'

'He asked me about my exams. He wanted to know when my last one was.'

'Why do you think he asked that?'

'Because he was planning something special for when they were finished.'

'What was that special thing he planned?'

'We all went for a family meal to Benni Roberto's. It was our favourite restaurant because it was all you can eat, but it was really hard to get a table. Dad obviously wanted to book one early.'

'How was the meal?'

'It was great.'

'I take it your exams went well?'

'Yeah. I got A's and B's.'

'How did you feel when you were in your exams?'

'Nervous.'

'How much revision did you do?'

'Quite a lot.'

'You could have done more?'

I nod my head.

'Why didn't you do more?'

'The headaches were bad.'

'After the accident?'

I nod again.

'What did it feel like when you came home from hospital?'

'Good.'

'What did it feel like when you were in hospital?'

'It was weird. I didn't like everybody fussing over me. And I remember it being loud.'

'Do you remember when the doctor spoke to you when you woke up?'

'Yeah.'

'What did he look like?'

'He had grey hair. He was a bit chubby.'

'Did he have glasses on?'

'Yes.'

'What about the paramedics who took you to hospital? What did they look like?'

I'm just about to tell Wendy that I don't remember because I could never remember anything between being at home after school and waking up in hospital when I suddenly get a glimpse of the park I was found in that night.

I'm sitting on a wall, looking out at the lights of the town before me.

And there's somebody sitting beside me.

I open my eyes and sit forward in the chair, breathing in hard and suddenly looking to Wendy as if to explain to me what just happened.

'It's okay,' she tells me, and I can feel her put her hand on my left one, which is gripping the arm of the chair.

'I remembered being in the park,' I say, almost in disbelief because this has never happened before.

'What did you see?'

'It was dark. All the lights were on around town. The park was empty. Except...'

*Who was the other person there with me?*

'Here, have some water,' Wendy advises me, and she hands me a plastic cup, which I gratefully receive.

The cold water is refreshing and helps soothe my throat, which has become surprisingly dry. But I don't want to spend too long enjoying it because I feel like I was on the verge of remembering something important then.

'I can't believe it,' I say, because it's true. All these years and I have never remembered anything in between being at home and being in hospital. Until today.

'Just relax. Take your time,' Wendy tells me, but that's easier said than done.

'Somebody was with me at the park,' I say. 'I couldn't see them, but I knew they were sitting beside me on that wall. I could feel it.'

'Here, let me take that for you,' Wendy says as she takes the empty cup and goes over to a side table where more water is waiting.

'What happened?' I ask her. 'What did you do?'

Wendy takes her time in answering me, instead seemingly more concerned with filling up another cup of water for me. Finally, she returns to her seat and hands me the cup before giving me an explanation.

'Usually when we recall an event from our past, we think chronologically,' she says as I take another thirsty gulp. 'We live our lives that way, so it makes sense that we think of things in that order. Start at the beginning and go to the end.'

'But we went to the end first?'

'That's right. Or at least a point past the night you are trying to recall. I was just looking for a good point to start from and work backwards. When you mentioned the surprise that your father was planning for after your exams, then I used that.'

I nod my head, understanding it, or at least on a very basic level. No doubt Wendy has spent years reading papers on the theory of this stuff.

'When you go backwards, it can trick your brain into working differently and recalling new things. Because you created the habit of always trying to remember that night chronologically, your brain knew which part you got stuck on and automatically skipped over it. But going backwards made it feel fresh.'

'Well, it worked.'

'Good. It doesn't always. But I thought it was worth a try.'

'Can we do it again?' I ask, glancing up at the clock behind Wendy's desk and seeing that there is still a little time left in the session, although I'm surprised to see that more time has passed than I realised. It had always been that way when I came here, though. One minute I'm saying hello to her, the next I'm wondering where the hour went.

'We can, but I prefer not to do it so close together,' Wendy says. 'But what I would like you to do is practise this when you are at home. Just lie down in bed, close your eyes and go back over things but start at a point after the accident and work backwards. Can you do that for me?'

I nod, feeling more confident than ever that I have a chance of regaining my memory.

We spend the next few minutes going through some more breathing exercises, a standard way to end our sessions, although, unlike all the previous times, I'm not feeling deflated. I'm feeling anxious to get home and do the exercise again. I will do it over and over until I remember more. Now I know that I wasn't alone in the park that night before I was found unconscious, I firmly believe the person who was with me is the person tormenting me now and the same person who has killed all those poor men.

Finally, after all this time, I might know what caused my accident. Finally, I might understand why I have to put up with my migraines. And finally, I might be able to figure out who the person from my past is before they can get to Tom.

## 39

I'm doing what Wendy advised me to do. Not only do I want to remember, but the police don't seem to be getting anywhere with finding out who is responsible for the murders and threats. Detective Rodgers and PC Brown seem like good men who are doing the best they can, but their best doesn't seem to be good enough. Every hour that passes is a nerve-shredding one as I wonder if this will be the hour when I receive another message on my phone with another ominous warning that makes me fear for Tom's life. So far, nothing has happened since the intruder entered our home three nights ago.

Everything has gone quiet.

Too quiet.

But quiet is also the way I need it to be if I am going to have a chance at recreating the state that Wendy got me into in her office yesterday. She told me to lie down on the bed, close my eyes, and think back to something that happened after my accident. Then I am to work backwards in time, just like she guided me in our session, until finally, I reach the night of the accident and hopefully remember something else.

I tried this in bed last night, and it didn't work.

Here I go again.

My eyes are closed, and my body is sinking into the mattress, although I'm on top of the duvet because I don't want my brain to think that I'm going to sleep because sleep won't help me here. I don't want a dream, I want an actual memory, so it's important that I stay awake. Sleep has been an elusive thing for me lately, so I don't think I have much to worry about there, but best not to take any chances.

As I lie still and run through the breathing exercises, I can hear how quiet the house is around me. Bless him, Tom has taken my request on board and is making as little noise as possible while I give this another go. I'm not sure if he genuinely believes it is going to help me remember, but he knows how important it is that I try. He could see how shocked I was when I came out of Wendy's office after that session when I remembered something, even if he was feeling a little perturbed that he hadn't been allowed to sit in on it. But remembering something isn't enough. I need to remember it all.

As the deep breaths work their magic, and I feel myself becoming more at ease, I begin the process. Yesterday when I tried this by myself, I used the same point in time that Wendy chose, the night when my father took me and the rest of my family out for a meal to celebrate the end of my exams. But that didn't work the second time, so I'm going to try something different. This time, I will start a few weeks after that, during one of my fun memories of my time with Shaun, my first boyfriend.

It had been a hot summer's day when the pair of us

had gone to a barbecue at one of our school friends' homes, joining several of our classmates as we enjoyed good food, great music and even a few sneaky beers when we could get away with it. The mood was high and not just because the sun was out in a part of the world that usually gets very little of it. Everyone was celebrating because school was over and we had our whole lives to look forward to. No more classes. No more teachers. No more exams. It was hard to see at the time how life could have got any better. But there was one way I saw for things to improve at that time. It was in my plan to set Nicola up with Shaun's best friend, Gareth.

The way I saw it, what could be better than my best friend getting into a relationship with Shaun's. Then we could go on double dates together and spend even more time in each other's company. I didn't see any flaws in my plan that day to get Nicola and Gareth together, although, in hindsight, there were plenty. I told Nicola to go and get Gareth a hot dog from the barbecue, which she did before the poor lad reminded her, and me, that he was a vegetarian. Then I told Gareth to go and get Nicola a drink, thinking he would get her something alcoholic, or at least fruity, but he came back with water, which was hardly the way to a woman's heart. And I constantly did my best to get the pair to sit near each other, often moving myself or Shaun so that we weren't getting in the way. But nothing worked. Despite my conviction that they would make the perfect couple, it was clear that their hearts weren't in it. But that doesn't matter now. All that matters is that the barbecue is my starting point.

Now I'll go backwards again and hopefully remember something else from the night of my accident.

I think about the day after my final exam when I woke up after a late night celebrating and needed Mum to drive me to the shops so we could get snacks. From there, I go back to the morning of one of the exams, when I was standing in the corridor with the rest of my classmates, riddled with nerves and doing my best to cram in some last-minute revision. Then I skip back a month to when I was in the hospital, sitting up in the bed and laughing as Nicola read me some of the funny tales from the trashy 'real-life stories' magazines she had found in her mum's wardrobe.

I'll never forget the one about the middle-aged woman who married her Hoover.

Now I'm getting close to the night of the accident, but before I get there, I recall the evening when my parents sat by my bed and held my hand as I cried, though they were more tears of stress than of pain. While my head hurt a little back then, what had felt worse was not being able to remember. I can still feel that sense of frustration, as well as all the times my dad told me that it was okay and that the only thing that mattered was that I was safe.

Then I go back again and pray that something else comes to me.

But it doesn't. I think back to the park, and I can see myself on the wall, just like where I got to in the session with Wendy, but there are no new memories forthcoming, and the more I try, the more unnatural it feels. As my brain scrambles for anything to latch onto, my next thought is of the afternoon of the accident, when I was at home after finishing school, looking forward to chilling out while the sounds of my dad's voice in his study floated up from downstairs.

That's it. I can't remember anything more about that night. It hasn't worked again. The first time must have been a fluke.

I open my eyes and let out a deep breath, frustrated

both at my brain's inability to remember what I need it to but also at myself for getting my hopes up and thinking this was going to work. Maybe I'm destined to never fully recall what happened to me. Perhaps it has nothing to do with willpower and is simply because the memory isn't there and never will be.

Before I know it, I can feel tears flowing from my eyes and rolling down my cheeks, and I'm at least glad that Tom isn't here, so he doesn't have to see me like this. I'll just stay in this dark room until I feel better again. Then I'll have to hope that the police have some news for us regarding the identity of the attacker because it's clear I don't have any.

The sound of the doorbell ringing disturbs the peace in the house, and I can hear Tom making his way to the front door. He had told me earlier that his dad was going to call around and drop some food off for us, which I know he is grateful for because I had suggested we get takeaway again even though it's all we've had lately.

I think about getting up and going downstairs to say hello, but I'm still feeling a little emotional, and I don't want Tom's dad to see that I have been crying, so I figure I'll just stay here. But then it hits me that it might seem rude, and I don't want to appear ungrateful to my future in-laws, so I decide to wipe my eyes quickly and get up off the bed.

I reach the bedroom door just as I hear Tom opening the front one, and I prepare myself for the booming voice of his father. He's a loud and chatty man, and even though Tom will probably tell him to be quiet because I'm resting upstairs, I don't think it's possible for him. But maybe I was wrong because I don't hear anything as I reach the top of the stairs and look down.

That's when I see Tom on his knees, holding his

stomach with his back turned to me. I have no idea what he is doing, and I'm just about to ask him when I see the figure step through the open doorway. They are wearing a balaclava. They are dressed all in black. And they have a knife in their hand.

A knife that is covered in blood.

'No!' I cry as I run down the stairs, my first instinct being to protect my fiancé before this masked intruder can strike another blow.

My reaction, or simply my appearance, must catch the attacker off guard because they take one look at me coming towards them before turning and running back outside.

As I reach the bottom of the stairs, I hear Tom gasping for breath, and that's when I see all the blood on the front of his T-shirt.

'Oh, my god!' I cry as I hold him and do what I can to help make him more comfortable.

His eyes look up at me, scared and shocked, and I wish there were something I could say to make this all better. But there isn't.

Seconds later, Tom's eyes are no longer open.

## 40

I always feared the time might come when I might have to say goodbye to Tom. What I had assumed was that it would be many years in the future before that happened. In the interim, I expected there to be all sorts of wonderful things that we would get to enjoy together. Of course, there was supposed to be a wedding and a honeymoon. Then we would have moved to a new house, buying somewhere bigger in anticipation of the family we wanted to have. Then would have come the pregnancies and the births, the tears and the tantrums, and all the wonderful memories as we raised what we had planned to be at least two little people into adulthood. After that, we would have looked to retirement, making plenty of plans to see more of the world in our golden years, as well as spending time with grandchildren as we grew older and the years started to catch up with us. Eventually, it would only have been a matter of time until one of us slipped away, and I always hoped it would be me first because even though it was selfish, I just couldn't bear the thought of being alone again so late in life.

All that time. All those years. All those memories.
Gone.

Now the doctor is on his way to confirm it to me.

I can barely bring myself to look at him as the doctor takes his seat opposite me while my parents and Tom's sit or stand nearby, nervous wrecks, exhausted, with tear-stained eyes. This is it. This is the moment I have been dreading ever since I saw Tom get loaded into the back of the ambulance outside our house while the neighbours gawked and gossiped.

*This is when the doctor will tell me that the love of my life has died.*

I try to focus as he speaks.

'Tom has lost a lot of blood, and he's not out of the woods yet, but he is stable, and we're confident he is going to be okay.'

It takes a moment for the words to sink in. 'He's okay?' I ask in complete disbelief.

'At the moment, yes,' the doctor tells us as Tom's parents hug each other tightly, and my mum weeps into my father's shoulder with relief.

I stare at the doctor for a few more seconds as if to double-check that he isn't winding me up, but he's not. Tom is okay. He didn't die on our doorstep, and he didn't die in that ambulance. He has survived.

'Can I see him?'

The doctor says yes, so I follow him quickly out of the waiting room and towards the ward where Tom is being looked after. As I go, I notice Detective Rodgers standing in the corridor, and he sees me, but before he can say anything, I raise my hand to signal that now is not a good time before I'm shown into Tom's room.

The sight of him lying in the bed with wires coming out of him and the heart rate monitor bleeping away is a sobering one, but it's certainly a better sight than the one that met me when I had looked down the stairs and saw him in pain.

'He's still sedated, so he won't be able to talk,' the doctor tells me, and I nod before rushing around to the side of the bed and taking my fiancé's hand. It feels cold, though thankfully not as cold as it felt when I was holding it on our doorstep in front of the open front door while the attacker ran away into the night.

The tears flow easily as I sit there and thank my lucky stars that Tom survived. I have no doubt that if I hadn't startled the attacker and ran towards them, then my partner would not be alive now. The masked figure had stepped towards Tom as he lay injured on the floor, and looked ready to finish him off before I appeared – I'm so glad that I chose to get up and leave the bedroom instead of staying on the bed.

I spend a grateful five minutes with Tom before letting his parents have a chance to see him, and as I step outside into the corridor again, this time I'm ready for Detective Rodgers.

'This is your fault!' I tell him before he can even get a word out. 'You should have protected him. I told you this person wasn't going to stop until everybody was dead.'

To be fair to him, the detective takes my anger without complaint, although I was ready for a fight if he was going to give me one. But he waits until I have calmed down before telling me that I need to make a witness statement about what I saw so that they can hopefully find the person responsible. But considering I didn't see much other than a balaclava, black clothes, and a knife, I'm not sure how helpful I am going to be.

Then Detective Rodgers says the other thing he came here to tell me. 'It's obviously not safe for you at your house anymore. Do you have anywhere else you could stay until we catch this person?'

'I don't know. I guess I could stay with my parents.'

'Okay, whatever you decide, I want you to know that we are going to have a police officer outside the property at all times to ensure your safety.'

I'm not sure if the detective is expecting me to thank him for that, but as far as I'm concerned, it's too little, too late.

'You should have had somebody protecting Tom so he wouldn't be in there right now!' I say, pointing in the direction of my fiancé's room and feeling the tears returning.

The detective looks sheepish and offers his best wishes before making a hasty departure but not before telling me that two officers are in the waiting room, ready to take my statement.

I take a few minutes to compose myself before I go and see them, sitting down on one of the uncomfortable plastic chairs that are fixed to the wall in this brightly lit corridor while holding my head in my hands. All the stress of the last few hours combined with the lack of quality sleep or food over the last few weeks has left me a broken woman, and I'm finding it tough to keep going. I just want all of this to be over, but it isn't.

What if the intruder tries to come back and finish Tom off? What if they are successful that time? And what if the police never find out who has done all of this?

I don't know if we will ever be safe again.

## 41

Tom's recovery is going well, but he still has a long way to go before he can go home. But that's fine by me because I feel the hospital is the safest place for him right now. Between the police officer standing guard outside his room and the dozens of doctors and nurses swarming around this place to provide medical assistance if needed, I am confident my fiancé is okay as long as he is in here. But he can't stay here forever. Eventually, he will be discharged, and then all bets are off. Even with the assurances of Detective Rodgers, I don't feel that the police are going to be able to stop whoever it is who wants my partner dead.

I rub my bleary eyes as I wait for the women in the hospital café to serve me my cup of tea before I carry it over to one of the tables and take a seat.

'That looks nice,' Nicola says, and I laugh at her sarcasm as I stir my spoon in the dull-coloured liquid before scooping out the tea bag and taking a sip.

'It tastes nice too,' I say before screwing up my face, and we laugh again, which is just what I need after spending most of the last week in this hospital, worrying about Tom. 'Are you regretting not getting one?'

'No, I'm good with my overpriced bottle of water, thanks.'

I smile as Nicola fiddles with her own drink before my mood returns to its dark state, and I start to worry again.

Fortunately, Nicola is on hand to pick me up quickly, which is what she has spent most of the last few days doing ever since she found out about what happened to Tom and came to visit us at the hospital.

'I think when all of this is over, we should have a double date,' she suggests, leaning back in her seat.

'Just one problem with that. You don't have a date.'

'Ahhh, that's where you're wrong. I am seeing some-body now, I'll have you know.'

'Really? Who?'

'He's called Simon. We met online, and we went for drinks last night.'

'Wow, I'm impressed.'

'I didn't want to say anything, but I figured it might help take your mind off things.'

'No, I'm glad you did. Just because my life is a mess, it doesn't mean other people can't be enjoying theirs.'

Nicola smiles, and I'm glad about that because I mean what I say. I don't want her to feel guilty for going on dates while I'm sitting at the hospital, worrying about my partner. Tom isn't her problem, and she deserves to be happy. It's nice to talk about her for a change too because I feel like we've done nothing but talk about my life lately, and it must be wearing her down almost as much as it's wearing on me.

'Do you think I could see Tom?' she asks me as I take another sip of my terrible tea.

'Of course,' I say, surprised because she hadn't asked

before and had always seemed happy just to make sure that I was all right. 'We can go now if you like.'

I'm happy for any excuse to leave my tea behind and get out of this dreary café, so I get up and lead Nicola through the rabbit warren of corridors that make up this hospital in the direction of Tom's room.

The sight of the police officer standing outside my fiancé's room is always a strange one, and Nicola's reaction to his presence highlights just how weird it is as we approach him.

'It feels like we're in a BBC crime drama or something,' she muses.

The policeman gives me a nod as I walk past him, and I offer him a small smile back, knowing that he's following orders and that it's not someone like him whom I should be mad at. It's a different story with Detective Rodgers though – I'm still angry at him for letting things escalate to this point.

Tom is sleeping when we walk in, as he was when I last left him, but I decide to give him a gentle nudge so he can wake up and say hello to Nicola.

As we take our seats beside him, and just before I give Tom a tap on the shoulder, I notice that my best friend is suddenly struggling to control her emotions.

'Are you okay?' I ask Nicola as she starts to cry.

'I'm sorry,' she says, wiping her eyes. 'I need some fresh air.'

Before I can stop her, Nicola has left her seat and rushed out of the room, leaving me sitting by the bed, wondering what has just come over her. I go after her to make sure she is okay, so leave quietly without waking Tom, probably making the police officer on the door wonder what we're up to.

I see Nicola heading for the entrance doors to the hospital and follow her outside, where several other visitors and patients are standing around, some of them smoking, some just soaking up a bit of the good weather that has come over the last days.

'Nic, are you okay?' I ask as I finally catch up to her.

'I'm fine. I'm just being silly,' she replies, dabbing at her eyes with a tissue.

'What's wrong?'

'It's just seeing Tom in there. It's so sad. And I thought about what it must have been like for you when you were waiting to find out what happened to him. It's just awful.'

'But he's okay now, and so am I,' I tell her before giving her a hug.

'Yeah, I know,' she says before blowing her nose. 'I think it's just hospitals. They've always made me feel weird.'

I can understand that. Looking around us right now at all the patients in gowns and the paramedics walking to and from their ambulances is enough to give anyone the creeps.

'I think I'm just going to go. Is that okay?' Nicola says.

'Of course. Whatever you want.'

We hug again before she walks away, and I watch her disappear across the car park before turning back to the doors and preparing to go back into the dreary building. But the feeling of the warm sun on my skin is welcome, so I decide to linger outside for a few more moments.

Taking a seat on one of the benches that isn't occupied by a smoker, I reach into my jeans pocket for my mobile phone and turn it on, deciding that this is a good opportunity to check it before I go back into a 'No Phone' zone.

I have barely had time to do anything with it before the message pops up on my screen.

*It was nice to see you the other night. Send Tom my best wishes. And I'll see you again soon.*

It's the mystery number again. The murderer. My tormentor. The person who has put my fiancé in this hospital.

I can't help it. I know I'm in a public place, but I don't care.

I throw my phone to the floor and let out a cry of frustration, one loud enough to make every smoker in this area choke on their cigarette.

## 42

A s visits to the family home go, this is about as weird as it gets.

I'm currently sitting in the living room of my parents' house, watching television with them and doing my best to make small talk while two police officers sit outside the house and keep watch to make sure that nobody is coming to harm us.

So far, we have managed to comment on the weather, the news report about the earthquake in Greece, and the fact that my father's car is due for its MOT and will have to go in next week. Basically, we are trying to talk about anything other than the fact that there is a psycho out there who killed all my exes, tried to kill Tom, and now might be thinking about killing me too.

But of course, it isn't working. No matter how many times Dad changes the channel or the topic of conversation, or how many cups of tea Mum offers to make me, I can't stop thinking about what might happen next. The text message yesterday was proof that this is far from over, if the fact that Tom had been stabbed in our home hadn't been enough evidence of that already. I informed Detective Rodgers as soon as I received it, and he immediately stepped up the security around Tom in the hospital ward, as well as telling me that I was not to return home and would have to stay somewhere else until they caught this person. I'd rather that place hadn't been my mum and dad's house, but I didn't have many options, and of the ones I did, this place is definitely the most secure. My parents own a large home outside Blackburn, surrounded by lovely green countryside, and the house sits behind a large electronic gate that I mocked my father for installing at the time but am now very glad for. The police car is parked in front of that gate, so that is two very big obstacles for any would-be intruder to have to get beyond, although I'm hoping the presence of the police car alone is enough to make anybody stay away.

I arrived here yesterday straight from the hospital, while PC Brown and a colleague went to my house and packed some belongings for me. I had done my best to give them a list of things I needed, but my emotional state and their apparent confusion over the difference between comfortable clothing and things I never wear means I haven't got everything I wanted. But that doesn't matter. My parents' home still contains enough of my old possessions to mean that I'm not going to struggle while I'm here, at least in that regard.

But mentally, this is proving to be a challenge.

'Just watch what you would normally watch,' I tell my dad after growing tired of his constant channel hopping as he attempts to find something that he thinks I might want to see. I know he is only trying to help me by taking my mind off things, but by acting unnaturally, he's just making me feel worse. Normally, my dad is the kind of guy who guards the television remote with his life and puts on whatever he wants, but now he is constantly offering me the remote and asking if I'm happy with what is on TV. But of course I'm not happy. I'm not happy with anything right now.

'Dad, seriously, this is fine,' I tell him as he continues to fidget beside me while changing the channels.

'When have you ever liked cooking shows?' he asks me as some celebrity chef stands over a sizzling pan on the screen.

'I'll watch anything. I don't care.'

'We can find something better,' he says and goes back to channel hopping again, causing me to grit my teeth and wonder how long I am going to have to stay here under these conditions.

'How about another cuppa?' Mum asks me, either noticing that I'm getting frustrated or simply that it's been ten minutes since she asked me for one.

'I think I'm going to have an early night,' I say, suddenly getting up from the sofa and heading for the door.

'It's only eight?'

'I'm tired. Goodnight.'

'Night, then.'

I feel bad about Mum and Dad as I leave the room and head up the stairs because I know they are trying to come to terms with this weird situation too, but right now, I need some space. Or rather, I need my fiancé.

I'm missing Tom terribly, and it's driving me mad that he's stuck in that hospital while I'm stuck here. Both of us are being protected by the police, but even with the increased security, I still feel like it won't be enough. Whoever is doing all of this is clearly persistent, and I fear that all the measures we are taking aren't going to be enough to stop whatever they want to do to Tom and me.

I just want to be at home, in my own house with the man I love, planning our wedding. Instead, I'm walking into my childhood bedroom while my fiancé is hooked up to all sorts of machines in a hospital ward and several coppers keep patrol around both of us.

This is not a normal life.

Slumping down onto the bed I spent years sleeping in as a child, I stare up at the ceiling and see the black mark on the paintwork that I caused when I was four-teen. I'd been standing on the bed and pretending to be a pop star, singing into the bottom of a broom handle as I imagined that I was performing on a stage for my thousands of adoring fans. In my exuberance, I got carried away and lifted the broom up quickly above my head, which was supposed to be for the benefit of 'the crowd' but only served to scuff the paint on the ceiling and leave a black mark, which is still there to this day. I'm not sure whether I should see it as a good or bad thing that it's still there. It's good because it reminds me of a happy memory. It's bad because it reminds me that my parents haven't redecorated in here ever since I offi-cially moved out, and now here I am, back in this room again, feeling like I've gone back in time.

But going back in time is what I need to do if I want to remember what happened that night in the park when I was sixteen. This is the last place I remember being before I woke up in that hospital bed. Other than the brief flashback to sitting on the wall in the park that night, being here was the only thing I could remember before everything went black.

*So maybe this is the place I need to be to jog my memory.*

Closing my eyes, I decide to have another go at the exercise Wendy did with me. All the stress and drama of the last few days means that I don't even bother with the breathing exercises to get me into a relaxed state. I'm exhausted enough that it happens anyway.

Picking another memory from after my accident, I work backwards again, moving non-chronologically through my past just like I was shown. The summer. The exams. The hospital. The flowers. The visitors. The doctor explaining what had happened.

And then I see it, another new memory of being in that park, sitting on that wall with somebody next to me. I turn towards them, and I know I'm seconds away from seeing who they are until I suddenly close my eyes.

Then I feel it. Their lips on mine. We're kissing. It feels good. Exciting. Unexpected.

Finally, our lips separate, and I open my eyes.

And then I see him.

The person I was with in the park that night. The only person who knows what caused my head injury.

I was right about it being someone from school.

It's Gareth.

Shaun's best friend.

**43**

## THE BOYFRIEND

I've always been in love with Adele Davies. She was going to love me too; I just know it. But then she banged her head, and she forgot all about me.

Until today.

I'm guessing the appearance of several police cars outside my flat this morning means that she has remembered that I was with her in the park that evening. Somehow, she must have recalled the memory from when she was sixteen, no doubt prompted to try again after I left her a clue in the form of the shattered school photograph. But that's okay. That's what I wanted to happen. She remembers me now, which means what I do next will not be as shocking for her.

As I watch the police officer heading towards my front door, I wonder if they are going to waste much time knocking before they barge their way in. Considering that I'm a murder suspect now, I doubt it. They'll want to get me in handcuffs as quickly as possible and haul me down to the station so that *they can begin questioning me and try to determine if there is any evidence linking me to the deaths of those five men Adele used to date. Then there's also the fact that they are having to use considerable resources to keep Adele and her fiancé safe while they look for the attacker, so with that in mind, I'm sure the police want this over just as quickly as the targets do.*

*I guess that's why the police only knock once before bursting through my front door and rushing into my property.*

*Fortunately, I'm not home at this time, so I won't be getting pushed against a wall and arrested on suspicion of anything. Instead, I'm watching from the window of the second flat I rented out before I started all of this, the one I knew would be safer to stay in just in case the police did come calling at my registered address. It's a good thing I did; otherwise I'd be being put into the back of a police car right now instead of getting to walk out of here and continue on with my plan to go and visit Adele this evening.*

*To say I'm excited to see her again is an understatement. Of course, I get to see her photo every day on social media by simply accessing her profile, but it will be great to be with her in person, just like it was great to be with her at Shaun's funeral. The sombre occasion to mark the passing of my best friend was a great opportunity to see Adele, and I'm glad she was in attendance. I hadn't been sure if she would think it appropriate to go to the funeral of her ex-boyfriend, but there she was, looking stunning in her black dress, and it was hard to concentrate on my speech without looking in her direction too many times as I spoke. It was even harder to talk about Shaun taking his own life when I knew that I was the one who had taken it instead.*

*Shaun had been my best friend all the way through secondary school. We shared everything. Our passion for football. Our interest in rock bands. And most of all, our taste in women.*

*I liked Adele first, and she liked me.*

*But it was Shaun who ended up being with her.*

*Things could and should have been so different if only fate hadn't intervened. That's because I had taken the initiative and told Adele that I liked her first. I did it by going to her house and getting her attention by throwing stones at her bedroom window. When she looked outside, I asked her if she wanted to come to the park with me. The bottles of alcopop I had stolen from my older brother's stash were the convincer, and while Adele told me she was supposed to stay in and revise, she ended up sneaking out and accompanying me to the park.*

*It was there where we sat on the wall overlooking town, sipping on our drinks and getting tipsy, while talking about all the things we were going to do after school was over. The travelling. The adventure. The freedom. We got on well, but then we always had. We had never been what people would consider friends, and our paths only really crossed on occasion in the classroom or at house parties, but I had always liked her, and I had the inkling that she would like me too if only I was to make my move.*

*That night in the park was my chance.*

*When we kissed, it was as perfect as I'd dreamed it would be. When we kissed again, I knew that Adele was enjoying herself as much as I was. And when we spoke about going on dates and maybe even letting people know that we were together now, I couldn't feel more excited for the future. I was sixteen, in love, and best of all, the object of my desire liked me too. It doesn't get much better than that.*

*Unfortunately, I was right.*

*That last moment as we sat beside each other on the wall was the last time I was ever truly happy. A second later, Adele had fallen backwards onto the concrete playground, losing her balance, and she banged her head and didn't wake up.*

*I did my best to help her. I called to her and shook her and begged her to open her eyes. But she didn't respond, and the more time that went by, the more I was convinced that she was dead.*

*Therefore, I panicked, gathered up the empty bottles of alcohol and left.*

*It turned out to be the biggest mistake of my life.*

*Adele lived but suffered memory loss, meaning that while I was off the hook for leaving her in the park, she had also forgotten about all the good things that had happened between us before her accident. The bonding. The laughter. The kisses. All of it was gone from her brain, and I knew that because it was the talk of school. Everybody was gossiping about Adele and what might have happened to her that night. Only I knew the truth, but I couldn't reveal it.*

*Because Adele would never have forgiven me for leaving her.*

*I'd thought that things couldn't get much worse than losing the girl I loved. But I was wrong. They could get so much worse, and they did, only a few weeks after Adele returned to school. That was because she started dating my best friend instead.*

*Seeing her with Shaun was gut-wrenching because I knew it should have been me who was enjoying all the affection from her, not him. That early time in my life should have been the best, growing into adulthood with feelings of love, lust and happiness but instead, I was consumed by jealousy, anger and sadness. The more time that went by, the worse I felt, but I had to keep it a secret from everybody, which only made me more withdrawn and left me feeling like I was half the person I used to be.*

*There was only mild relief when Shaun told me that Adele had ended things with him when they were eighteen. While I no longer had to suffer in seeing their relationship, I knew that my chance to get with Adele had gone. She was out of Blackburn and living life as a university student, while I was left stuck at home, bitter and frustrated at how things had turned out for me.*

*Those feelings never left, not even as the years ticked by and we all got older. I blame social media for that. I knew the healthy thing for me to have done was not follow her online accounts, but I did it anyway, constantly checking for updates to find out where she was and what she was up to. That was how I learnt about all the different boyfriends she had after Shaun, tormenting myself by staring at their happy photos on my phone and never losing that sense of injustice that it should have been me smiling beside her and not those other men.*

*I had relationships of my own over the years, and I did genuinely try to move on, but none of the women ever matched up to what I felt with Adele that night in the park. The more time that went by, the more obsessed I became with that belief until I started to direct my hate at the only people I could.*

*The men who had been with Adele instead of me.*

*Starting with Shaun and working all the way through to Jesse, I eliminated each and every one of them, not because they were love rivals in the present but because they had robbed me of so much of my happiness in the past. As each one was removed, I felt better about myself until only Adele's current partner was standing in my way of future bliss. But he survived my attack, although I will get him the next time that I have the chance. I'm not going to stop until Adele sees how much I love her and how much I have been willing to do to prove it.*

*But now I'm almost out of time. If the police are looking for me, then she has remembered that I was with her in the park that night. She must have given my name as a suspect, and now here they are, looking for me and hoping to end my reign of terror on this sleepy town. But it's not going to work.*

*It's taken me twenty years to act on all my feelings of helplessness, but now that I have, I'm almost there.*

*The only thing I need to do now is convince Adele that I am the only man she ever really needed.*

*To do that, I'm going to have to see her.*

*Face to face.*

*Tonight.*

**44**

---

I spent most of today either sitting with Tom by his hospital bedside or asking the police officer guarding his room if there was any news about their search for Gareth. While the time I spent with my fiancé was enjoyable as we made plans for our future and completed a sudoku puzzle in the newspaper, the time spent speaking with the police was not. They told me that they still haven't been able to find Gareth and are still unable to determine if he is the person responsible for all the heinous crimes that have ruined so many lives.

Remembering who I was with in the park that night was a shock, although I still don't know how I came to be found lying unconscious and in urgent need of medical attention. But I have to assume that Gareth knows and potentially was the reason behind it happening. Did he attack me and leave me for dead? I don't know for sure, but all the signs are pointing towards that conclusion.

Of the many surprising things about the memory recollection of that night when I was sixteen was the fact that Gareth and I kissed in the park. That means that I must have liked him enough at the time to do so, yet after the incident, I ended up dating his best friend for the next two years. Is that why he hates me? Is that why he killed Shaun, as well as everybody else who came after him?

Is that why Tom still requires around-the-clock protection?

I sat with Detective Rodgers and ran through all of the permutations of what each of them could mean as soon as I had remembered being with Gareth that night, and while much remained unclear, one thing did interest him. Based on what I told him, it seemed to give Gareth a motive. The fact that Gareth was also in the photo that was smashed in my home the other night only added to my belief that he was the guilty party. Those things combined was enough for the detective to send several police officers to Gareth's address in an attempt to bring him in for questioning.

Unfortunately, Gareth wasn't home, and they haven't had any luck tracking him down. That means I'm still sitting in a chair at my parents' house while a police car sits outside to protect us. How long is this going to go on for? Will it ever end?

Will the police find Gareth before he finds me?

The loud knock on the front door almost causes me to spill my cup of tea, the one my mum insisted on making for me even though I told her that I was okay.

'Who the hell is that?' my dad grumbles as he goes to get up out of his armchair.

'Wait! You have to be careful!' I tell him, standing up too and stopping him before he can get to the door. 'How do we know who it is?'

'Whoever it is had to get past the coppers on the gate, so I think we'll be okay.'

'Are you sure?'

'We have to answer it. It might be about Tom,' he tells me, but I'm terrified of something bad happening when we do. After all, the last time I heard a knock at the door, I went downstairs to find my fiancé clutching a stab wound to his stomach.

'Be careful,' I say as my mother and I follow him to the door, where we all take a deep breath before he opens it.

The sight of PC Brown standing on the doorstep is a relief, and we all step back to allow the officer inside before quickly locking the door again and returning to the safety of the warm living room.

'Have you found him?' I ask before anyone can take a seat.

'No, not yet,' PC Brown replies, shaking his head. 'We've tried his home address, as well as his work one, but haven't been able to locate him. We've also spoken to members of his family, and they say they haven't seen or heard from him in the last twenty-four hours.'

'What does that mean?'

'Well, considering people generally don't vanish for long periods of time, I'd say it means that there's a good chance he's our guy, and he's hiding.'

'What if he's not hiding? What if he's planning to come here?'

'We have the place well protected.'

'What about the back?'

'I'm sorry?'

'There aren't any officers watching the back of the house. And what if he comes over one of the side walls or the hedges?'

'Adele,' my father says, probably embarrassed that his daughter is casting doubt on a police officer's ability to do his job, but I don't let him knock me off my stride.

'If Gareth has been able to do all of this and get away with it for so long, what makes you confident you can stop him doing anything more?'

PC Brown hesitates to answer, and that's all the confirmation I need before the wave of dread that has threatened to consume me on more than one occasion recently returns to haunt me again.

'Why don't you go and have a lie-down?' my mum suggests rather condescendingly, as if I'm some batty woman who needs looking after before she makes a fool of herself.

'I'm fine!' I snap back, even though I feel, and probably look, anything but.

'Rest assured we are doing everything in our power to ensure that you and your family are safe, as well as Tom at the hospital,' PC Brown tells me, looking like he already needs some fresh air even though he only walked in here a moment ago.

'So what are you doing now?' I ask him. 'Have you got any idea where Gareth might be?'

'We're doing everything we can, and we will find him,' PC Brown replies, but that's still not good enough. Unfortunately, I can tell that is as good as it's going to get for tonight, so it seems I have two choices. Either stand here and protest some more or take my mother's advice and go and have a lie-down.

'Call me as soon as you find him,' I say to the police officer, who must surely be relieved when he sees me turn and walk out of the room.

I head upstairs, fed up, frustrated and feeling that there is no end in sight from the hell I have been living in for the last few weeks. All I want is for Tom to be back to full health and for the both of us to be able to return to our own home, where we can get on with the rest of our lives. But we can't do that with all this hanging over our heads. The police protection. The jumping at every knock at the door. And the knowledge that we're not the ones in control here.

I close my bedroom door and walk over to my bed, looking down at the duvet but not feeling like I want to get under it yet.

My laptop is sitting on top of it from when I was using it earlier, and I scoop up the end of the charger cable and plug it in, remembering that the battery died on me earlier. I had wasted a couple of hours watching some trashy reality shows online in a bid to take my mind off things, but it didn't really work. And I'm not sure anything I can come up with now is going to work either.

I'm tired, but I can't sleep. I'm bored, but I can't do anything. I'm angry, but I have nobody to take it out on. At least nobody who deserves it.

The one person who does is the one person who can't be found right now. Where is Gareth? What is he doing? And what does he want?

I imagine it's going to be a while before I find out.

But I'm wrong.

The hand that goes over my mouth stops me from screaming before the voice in my left ear tells me that I haven't found Gareth.

Instead, he has found me.

## 45

I've promised my captor that I won't scream when he removes his hand from my mouth, and I keep my word. That way, perhaps he will keep his word when he said he wouldn't be forced to hurt me if I was to call for help. Now we have passed the first test of trust, it's time to find out what is going to happen next.

'Take a seat on the bed,' Gareth tells me, the knife in his left hand convincing me that I'd better do as he says.

As I lower myself onto the duvet, Gareth sits down beside me, uncomfortably close, but then again, there isn't really any distance that I would feel safe sitting beside a man with a deadly weapon.

'What do you want?' I ask him, doing my best not to look as petrified as I feel.

'What do you think I want?'

'I don't know.'

'Isn't it obvious? After all this time and everything I've done?'

I keep my eyes on the carpet in front of us, my body still but my mind racing with fantasies of escaping this room before he can kill me.

'I want you, Adele,' he says after a moment. 'That's all I ever wanted.'

The fact that he was hiding in my bedroom with a knife could have told me that, but it's still weird to hear him say it.

'I don't understand. We've barely seen each other since school.'

'Not in person. But I have seen plenty of you. I have been watching you closely. I've never stopped seeing you, thanks to the internet.'

'You've been stalking me?'

'No, that's not the word I would use at all.'

Gareth looks agitated at my description of his behaviour, so I make a mental note not to use that word again.

'Then what have you been doing?'

'I've been admiring you, Adele. Like any boyfriend would.'

'Boyfriend? What are you talking about?'

Gareth puts one hand on my leg, and I do my best not to flinch or pull away, aware that any sudden movement on my part could get a quick reaction from his other hand – the one with the knife in it.

'I would have been your first boyfriend. I know you don't remember, but it's true. If it hadn't been for your accident, then you wouldn't have forgotten all about me, and you would never have got with all those other men instead.'

'Accident?'

'Yes, you banged your head.'

'Did you do it?'

My desire to want to run is almost matched by my desire to know the full story of what happened in the park that evening. Maybe if I call for help or make a run for the door, I could get a few seconds of freedom before he used the knife. I'll probably die, or maybe I'd get lucky and survive. But I'd never know what happened twenty years ago.

'Of course I didn't do it. I would never hurt you,' Gareth says.

'Then what happened?'

'We had gone to the park, where I'd told you how much I liked you. You have no idea how long I had waited to pluck up the courage to say that to you. I'd been drinking for an hour before I even met you just to make myself feel more confident. You were drinking too, remember? Almost as much as me in the end.'

I obviously don't remember, but I say nothing.

'Things went well. Even better than I had expected. You said you liked me too. I knew you wouldn't have felt as strongly as I did for you at the time, but I knew that would come. The important thing was that you didn't run away. And you didn't. Instead, you stayed, and you kissed me.'

I remember the kiss, the flashback hitting me after the memory exercise. But I only care about knowing what happened next.

'I don't understand. If everything went well, how did I end up in hospital?'

Gareth suddenly removes his hand from my leg and stands up, pacing the carpet in front of me, clearly distressed about this next part of the story. He's blocking my path to the door now, but I'm not going to run anyway. I need to know what happened.

'It was such bad luck. Such rotten, evil luck. You were the girl of my dreams, and you liked me back. I had everything a sixteen-year-old boy could have wanted. And then it all changed, just like that.'

Gareth clicks his hands and stops walking, looking at me with an expression he hasn't shown since he broke in here and threatened me in my childhood bedroom.

He no longer looks determined or dangerous.

He just looks sad.

'We'd had so much to drink, and we were having a great time. I was telling jokes and making you laugh. But then you got the giggles. I mean, really got them. You couldn't stop laughing. It was cute. But then you rocked your head back and lost your balance. You fell off the wall and banged your head on the ground.'

I stare at Gareth, mainly to try to see if he is telling me the truth. But I can see that he is. He looks so sad about it.

'It really was an accident?' I ask.

Gareth nods. 'A stupid accident. But it ruined everything.'

'What did you do?'

Gareth takes a moment to answer me, and it's obvious he feels ashamed about what his answer is going to be.

'I thought you were dead. Honestly, I did. If I'd known you were still alive, then I would have stayed and helped you, but I panicked.'

'You just left me?'

He says nothing.

'How could you do that?'

'I'm sorry. You have to forgive me,' he says, dropping to his knees and taking one of my hands, as if there is any way I could even entertain the idea of forgiving him. 'I was young. I was drunk. I didn't know what to do.'

Getting the answer to the question that has haunted me for years is not as much of a relief as I thought it would be, although it's probably to do with the fact that I had a crazy guy in my room when I got it.

I quickly decide there are two ways I can play this. Either I get mad at him for leaving me in the park that night. Or I tell him I forgive him and pretend like he still has a chance with me.

'It's okay, I understand. You were scared.'

Gareth smiles, and I can tell I chose the right option.

'I wanted to go and see you in the hospital and tell you what happened. I really did. But I was worried you would hate me, and I couldn't bear the thought of that.'

'I wouldn't have hated you,' I say, just telling him anything he wants to hear so he lowers his guard enough for me to get out of this situation.

'I know that now. But I was stupid at the time, and I just kept quiet. But then it was too late. You got out of hospital, and you came back to school, and that's when I saw it. I saw that you didn't remember me. You had completely forgotten that we had kissed that night.'

I see tears in Gareth's eyes, and he lowers his head for a moment, making me entertain the idea of hitting him and running for the door. But I can't guarantee the success of that plan, so I stay still for now.

'And then you got with him,' he says coldly, his demeanour changing instantly and the sadness in his eyes being replaced with a burning anger. 'You got with my best friend.'

'What did you do to him?' I ask, terrified of the answer.

'I got rid of him, just like I got rid of all the others. I only wish I'd done it sooner. Have you any idea what it was like to see you with all those men over the years, smiling for the camera and sharing the soppy status updates? It should have been me you were with. It should have been me in those photos.'

'It was twenty years ago,' I try, but it's clear that's the

wrong thing to say when Gareth looks at me with pure venom.

'It doesn't matter how long ago it was. You liked me first. You liked me before all the others. I was the one you should have been with.'

'Why didn't you tell me you liked me sooner? Why wait all these years?'

'I couldn't do it. I lost my nerve, and then you were with Shaun. By the time that ended, you'd left Blackburn and were at uni. Every time I hoped you would come home, you just kept travelling. Then it had been too long. I knew you'd think I was mad if I ever told you I liked you then. So I didn't. I tried to move on. I even had a few girlfriends. But I could never stop thinking about you. Never.'

Gareth's heartfelt speech is obviously years in the planning, and there is a tiny part of me that can see his pain and understand it. But none of it excuses what he has done.

'Why kill them? Why stab my fiancé? You had no right to do those things.'

'And you had no right to forget me!'

It's obvious that Gareth is becoming more frustrated now, and I need to change tactics. But before I can…

'Adele? Is everything okay up there?'

The sound of my dad's voice from the bottom of the stairs is both reassuring and frightening. Before I can answer, Gareth has his hand over my mouth again to stop me calling for help, although I'm not even sure I want to because I don't want to put my parents in danger as well.

'Tell him you're fine,' Gareth whispers to me. 'Or I'll slit your throat.'

I nod my head as he holds the blade in front of my face before he removes his hand.

'I'm fine, Dad,' I call back, even though I'm anything but.

Gareth waits for a moment to ensure no one is coming up the stairs before he sits down again beside me on the bed.

'What are you going to do?' I ask him, wondering how this situation can ever be resolved without one of us losing everything.

'I'm hoping I don't have to do anything,' he replies calmly. 'It's you who has a decision to make.'

'What do you mean?'

'I told you how much I liked you in the park twenty years ago. And I think I've proven it again now with my recent actions. All I ever wanted was to be with you. Now I need to know if you want to be with me.'

I stare at the man beside me, almost in disbelief about how delusional he is. Does he honestly think there is a future in which he and I are together? I'm guessing so; otherwise he wouldn't be here.

But I can't bring myself to say it, even though I know it's what he wants to hear and what is best to keep me safe. Not after what he has done to me, to Tom, and to all my poor exes.

'You're right, I did like you that night twenty years ago,' I say, my heart rate escalating fast as I prepare to risk everything. 'But not anymore. Now I can't stand the sight of you. So just do what you've got to do.'

Calling the bluff of a madman is obviously a risky game, but if he cares about me anywhere near as much as he has made out, then he won't be able to do it.

He won't be able to harm me.

'Adele, you don't mean that.'

'Yes, I do. You stabbed my fiancé. You killed all those poor men. And you left me to die when I was sixteen. How could I love a man like you?'

I see Gareth's fist clenching around the knife handle and know I'm making him angrier, but he's not the only one feeling that emotion.

He's also not the only one with a weapon.

Reaching behind me, I yank the charger cable from my laptop and hook it over Gareth's head before pulling as hard as I can. The surprise of my sudden movement, coupled with my desperate act of strength, causes us to tumble off the bed and onto the carpet – and he loses the knife as he hits the floor.

But I don't loosen my grip on the cable, continuing to choke him as he scrambles to break free.

'Dad! Help!' I call out now that I'm sure Gareth is disarmed.

I hear my father's footsteps bounding up the stair-case as I continue to pull the cable around Gareth's neck, and by the time Dad bursts into the room, Gareth has stopped struggling and fallen quiet.

'Oh, my god, Adele!' Dad cries as he takes in the sight of me lying on my bedroom floor with a charger cable wrapped around the neck of the intruder, but I refuse to release my grip until I am absolutely certain that Gareth is either dead or unconscious.

He left me that night when he assumed I was dead.

But I'm not leaving him tonight.

Not until I know for sure that he really is gone.

# EPILOGUE

R ed is the colour of romance, lust, and passion, but I consider white to be the colour of love. That's the colour of the cloths on the tables on which sit all the flowers, the wine bottles and the porcelain plates with the shiny cutlery. It's the colour of the drapes that are hanging over all the walls in this large room filled with over one hundred family and friends. And it's the colour of the dress I am wearing as I sit at the head of this room beside the man I love, whom I can now finally call my husband.

To say this wedding has been a long time in the making would be an understatement. As if it wasn't hard enough trying to decide on every detail that goes into pulling off a momentous event like this one, try dealing with a psychopathic figure from the past too. That's what Tom and I had to contend with before we could end up sitting here side by side at the top table while all our guests clink their champagne flutes together and toast to our future happiness.

It's a relief to be here now, not just because it means the end of all the wedding planning. It's proof that despite the terrible events that befell us, nothing has been able to break apart what will now be my last-ever romantic relationship. All the lies, the secrets, the forgotten memories, not to mention the murders and manhunts, could not stop me walking down that aisle and saying 'I do' to the man I love, a man who survived an attempt on his life and came back stronger.

I thought the joy of today would top anything I had experienced in my life, but as good as it has been, it still doesn't live up to the happiness I felt when Tom was discharged from the hospital after recovering from his stab wound. By then, there had been no need for a police officer to stand guard nearby because the person who had put him in hospital was in one himself. While Tom got to come home and put his feet up with me, Gareth was lying in a hospital bed, recovering from when I almost strangled him to death with a laptop charger, while two officers stood outside his room and kept watch. He was their prisoner now, and after the recent court case was concluded, he will continue to be imprisoned for at least the next twenty-five years.

Gareth pled guilty to the murders of Shaun, Calum, Ryan, Ash, and Jesse, and – even though it had been painful to do it – I had watched the entirety of the trial of the man who was dangerously obsessed with me via video link from a separate location. I heard about how Gareth had lured Shaun to the woods one day on the pretence of a friendly walk before strangling him with a rope and hanging him from the tree to make it look like suicide. I heard about how he had tampered with the brakes on Calum's car, causing him to lose control of his vehicle and veer off the road. I heard how he had travelled down to Ryan's home on the south coast and started the house fire that claimed his life. I heard about how he had followed Ash home after a night out and beaten the poor man to death in an alleyway. And lastly, I heard about how he had visited Jesse's home not long after Tom had been there himself, stabbing my last boyfriend to death and clearly getting some practise in for what was to come with Tom.

I had also heard again how Gareth had been obsessed with me since he was sixteen, all the way up until the recent night when he had snuck into my parents' home via the back garden, evading the police and threatening my life before I was able to subdue him. He also admitted to the court about leaving me that night in the park, a time when I could have easily died but somehow lived, although not without suffering the after-effects of terrible migraines and the blind spot in my memory that had tormented me for years.

The only part I hadn't been able to listen to was when Gareth had been told to recount the night when he had visited my home and stabbed Tom in the door-way. That was one memory I never wanted to hear recalled.

But now it is all over. Gareth is behind bars while I'm planning on spending the rest of today standing in front of one. This is a party, after all, and I'm looking forward to celebrating with all the people who have made me the woman I am.

Along with Tom and our parents, I can see Nicola sitting on the nearest table to ours, laughing away with all of the other bridesmaids and already looking a little worse for wear from all the free wine she has been glug-ging since lunchtime. I can see Wendy, the woman who helped me remember my past and got me to point the police in the direction of Gareth, and I'm glad we put her onto the guest list. And I can also see Rachel, my wedding planner, standing at the back of the room and surveying the scene to ensure that everything is running as smoothly as it should be. I'm glad she accepted my apology for the way I treated her that day when I thought she was behind the messages, and not just because Heron's Barn was one of the few venues within fifty miles that could cater to us today. It's also because we have since become good friends again, rekindling that companionship that once saw us as best friends before we drifted apart.

Things really couldn't be any better, in all areas of my life.

That's why I decide to follow the advice my mother gave me just before we left the hotel room this morning, which was to 'enjoy every second and take it all in.' I intend to do just that, and while much of what has led to this moment has been a whirlwind of vows, photographs, and speeches, I am going to make the most of this little moment right here.

Sitting back in my seat, I look at the people sitting either side of me and smile, knowing that I'll never be as loved by anyone as much as the people that are with me right now. Along with Tom, his parents and my mother, I can see my father finishing his dessert, and I smile at the lovely words he gave half an hour ago during his particular speech. He talked about love and loss, of how important it was to find that one true love and, most of all, how important it was to hold onto that person when you do. I made sure to listen to his advice in that respect, and I fully plan on holding onto the man I love for the rest of my life, which hopefully has many years to go yet.

Then I look out across the room at the sea of smiley faces sitting in front of me, and I see couples mixed in with singletons, all of them happy in different ways but all of them having one thing in common. They just want to be loved. But everybody has a different journey before they get to that goal.

Relationships blossom, and relationships fall apart. New sparks ignite, and old flames burn out. Nobody can predict it. And maybe that's for the best.

I don't want to know what the future holds.

The past was crazy enough for me.

## ABOUT THE AUTHOR

Did you enjoy The Boyfriend? Please consider leaving a review on Amazon to help other readers discover the book.

Daniel Hurst writes psychological thrillers and loves to tell tales about unusual things happening to normal people. He has written all his life, making the progression from handing scribbled stories to his parents as a boy to writing full length novels in his thirties. He lives in the North West of England and when he isn't writing, he is usually watching a game of football in a pub where his wife can't find him.

Want to connect with Daniel? Visit him at his website.

www.danielhurstbooks.com.

Published by Inkubator Books
www.inkubatorbooks.com

Made in the USA
Las Vegas, NV
21 October 2023

79443833R00157